Timmy and the K'nick K'nocker Ring

To Linda—
thanks for
your smiles.

Prismatic Publishing
2230 Sunset Blvd #330-190
Rocklin, CA 95765

Distributed by Simplie Indie, a Division of Prismatic Entertainment, Inc.
www.SimplieIndie.com

ISBN-13: 978-0-9846043-3-3
ISBN-10: 0-9846043-4-0

First Edition: July 2010
Cover art by C. Walker
Cover design by Bud Spencer, SUMO Graphics

Printed in the United States of America

Timmy and the K'nick K'nocker Ring

Written and Illustrated by:
Connie A. Walker

Dedicated to my grandchildren

Heartfelt gratitude is extended to my models:
Jennifer, Natasha, Nicholas, and Jonathan,
with special thanks to Seth,
who posed for all of the pictures of Timmy,
including the one where he is dangling upside down.

Table of Contents

Chapter 1
A Rotten Morning

As soon as I looked out my window that October morning, I knew I was headed for trouble. The ground was sparkly with frost, and I'd left my jacket at school the day before.

At the breakfast table I gobbled down a bowl of cereal and then sat stirring the last few flakes with my spoon. I hoped Mom would get a phone call or something so I could sneak out.

"Mindy asked me to go to the mall with her this afternoon," said my sister Brittney, who's in junior high.

"You're still grounded," Mom told her.

Brittney started whining and arguing.

I jumped up to take advantage of the distraction. If I hadn't left *Murphy's Fifth Grade Arithmetic* in the living room, I would've made it. I was stuffing the book into my backpack with one hand while I opened the front door with the other.

Then the voice of doom caught up with me.

"Timothy Alan Parker, where is your coat?"

Busted!

I turned around, and there was Mom with her fists on her hips and a scowl on her lips.

"I guess I left it at school yesterday."

"It's too cold to go outside without a coat," Mom said. She marched over to the hall closet.

Watching her with dread, I lost track of the front door. It slammed into my elbow as it swung shut. With a yelp, I dropped my backpack. Out tumbled the math book. It was followed by my pencils, string, chewing gum, homework (slightly crumpled), large pink eraser, rubber ball, and harmonica.

As I scooped up the mess, I kept my eyes on Mom. She pulled a tan jacket out of the closet and gave it a couple of shakes.

"You can wear Sam's old coat."

"Mom," I wailed, "the kids tease me enough already."

"Well, you just ignore them," she said without a hint of sympathy. "I don't want you getting sick just because a few children make rude remarks. Remember the old saying: 'Sticks and stones may break my bones, but words can never hurt me.'"

Right, I thought, *but Buck Peterson sure can.*

She handed me the coat. Then she stood with her arms folded and her toe tapping on the floor. "Put it on."

I leaned my backpack against the wall and shoved my arms into the sleeves.

"I can't wear this. Look!" I stretched my arms straight out in front of me. The cuffs hung down three inches beyond my fingertips.

My older brother, Sam, is a sophomore in high school and already on the football team. He probably wore this jacket in third grade. He's always been the biggest, tallest, strongest boy in his class. He takes after our father.

Me, I take after some distantly related pygmy.

Mom tucked the cuffs under, adjusted the shoulder seams, and zipped up the front. "There are poor children all over the world who would be grateful to have a coat this nice to wear." She took a step back and looked me over. "It's not too bad, and it'll remind you not to forget your jacket again. You'd better get going, or you'll be late."

There are times when I can wheedle my way around Mom and times I can't. Right now, she was angry at Brittney and not likely to take any mouthing off from me.

Without another word, I picked up my backpack. I stomped out the door and down the front steps to the sidewalk. As soon as I was past our neighbor's house, I stopped and yanked off Sam's coat.

"I'm going to tell Mom," Brittney shouted from behind me.

I hadn't heard her come out of the house. I spun around and glared at her. It was her fault that Mom was in a bad mood.

"Go ahead," I yelled back. "I'll tell her why you and Mindy always want to hang out at the mall."

I made a smooching sound on the back of my hand.

Then I imitated Brittney's voice, high and squeaky. "Oh, Jerry Fitzgerald at the Burger Barn is so dreamy. He's so cute."

I puckered up my mouth and kissed the air.

"Kissy, kissy, kiss."

"You little—!" She started for me, but Mindy's mother drove up just then and honked the horn. Brittney stuck her nose in the air and climbed into the car. Since starting junior high, Brittney, Mindy, and their friends think they're too cool to ride the school bus, so the mothers take turns driving them back and forth.

As they pulled away, Brittney poked her head out of the car window. "If you say a word to Mom, you are so totally dead."

"Oh, I'm scared." I grabbed my throat, stuck my tongue out the corner of my mouth, and gurgled like I was strangling myself. It was a wasted performance.

Mindy's mother was burning rubber, trying to catch the green light at the bottom of the hill.

I shivered.

No one else was around so I put Sam's jacket back on.

I hate wearing Sam's hand-me-downs, even when they fit. But having to wear something that drowned me just wasn't fair. I wanted to toss the blasted thing into the neighbor's garbage can, but I knew Mom would check to make sure I brought both jackets home. Besides, I was cold.

All I could do was hope that Buck Peterson didn't see me. Even the sixth graders steer clear of Buck. He's the meanest bully in the whole school, and he isn't afraid of anyone.

Every day he backs some poor kid into a corner and holds out his hand. He doesn't say anything, but the kid better have something—money, electronic game, cell phone, or maybe comic books—that Buck wants. If not, Buck'll beat him into a bloody mess. He's responsible for the loss of a lot of teeth, both baby and permanent. If someone rats on him so he gets sent to the principal, Buck doesn't care.

When the principal calls Buck's father in for a conference, nothing changes. Buck just laughs and does whatever he wants. Maybe his father's afraid of him too.

The chilly morning got even colder. A few clouds drifted in front of the sun, and a breeze whipped out of the north.

I shivered again and rubbed my arms with my hands like I've seen people do in the movies to keep warm.

It's amazing how much it doesn't help.

Chapter 2
Double Surprise

I knew in my gut that the day would only get worse.

I kicked a rock and watched it bounce along the sidewalk. I jogged up and kicked it again. It landed in the gutter. I went and got it, set it down, pulled back my foot, squinted, aimed, and gave it a boot. The rock bounced off a tree.

Not bad, I told myself.

If I tried, I was pretty sure I could hit the stop sign at the end of the block.

Missed.

Missed again.

One more try. One more. Just one more.

"Got it," I crowed out loud.

I started walking again.

Thomas Jefferson Elementary School was on the next corner.

I stopped and looked around. Where were the other kids? A glance at my watch and I knew.

9:05! Dang. Late.

I glanced at the school and shrugged.

Then I turned around and crossed the street. I was already going to get a tardy notice. Another few minutes wouldn't matter.

The neighborhood park has a narrow creek running down one side. There are three swings, a jungle gym, a dozen tires buried halfway in the sand, a slide, and a teeter-totter. Between the play area and the stream is an enormous old tree.

It was one of my favorite places, especially when no one else was around.

Dry autumn leaves of red and gold crunched under my feet. The air filled with a musty tang as I shuffled through them, stirring up little cyclones of dust.

There were two wooden benches underneath the tree's bare branches. I sat down on one and watched water trickle over the stones in the bottom of the creek bed.

Mom didn't understand how awful it was to be the shortest, skinniest boy in fifth grade—maybe in the whole school, not counting kindergartners. Everyone picked on me, not just Buck Peterson. I didn't have any friends. Not since Jimmy Grayson moved away last summer. After a moment, I pulled the harmonica from my backpack. Putting it to my mouth, I played a sad, lonely tune.

Music is my only talent. I can play almost any instrument by ear. My folks call it a gift. But it doesn't make me popular. Most kids in fifth grade spend more time figuring out how to ditch their music lessons than they spend practicing.

Behind the tree's broad trunk I heard a scuffling sound. I thought it was probably a squirrel kicking through the leaves just as I had.

In a few minutes, I found out how wrong I was.

A beam of yellow sunlight snuck around the clouds and flickered across the stream. It made the water sparkle, and below the surface, I noticed something glittery.

I stopped playing.

What is it? I leaned forward. *Oh, it's just a bit of old copper wire.*

No. I peered closer. *It's too shiny.*

Standing up, I put away my harmonica and pulled the straps of my backpack up over my shoulders.

With one foot on the bank and the other on a jagged rock, I bent and picked up the bright object.

It's a ring!

I held it up to the light. The band was gold and had strange symbols engraved around the inside. A tiny gem flashed red.

"What's that?" Buck Peterson shouted, jumping from behind the tree. His big, meaty hands tried to snatch the ring from me.

"Hey!" I blurted out, startled.

My foot on the rock slipped.

I swayed forward. I swayed backward.

I shifted my weight and tried to catch my balance.

I leaned to the right. I leaned to the left.

My foot slid out from under me.

Splash!

I landed on my rear end in about five inches of water.

"Ho, ho, ha, ha!" laughed Buck Peterson. "That was great. Do it again."

With my jeans dripping and my shoes and socks soaked, I sloshed my way over to the bank across from him.

Darn that Buck Peterson!

Now I'd have to go home and change clothes.

Mom would be so mad.

Hmmmm. Well, maybe not.

If I showed her the ring, maybe she'd forget I fell into the creek instead of going to school. Maybe the ring would turn out to be worth a lot of money. We could sell it and become millionaires.

Maybe I wouldn't have to go to school at all today.

Sure, when pigs fly.

I looked at the ring again and sighed. Even if it was solid gold, even if the gem was a real ruby, the darned thing was so little it couldn't be very valuable.

I might as well toss it away.

"What have you got?" Buck demanded. "Give it to me, you stinking little hobbit." He took a few steps back so he could get a running start to jump over the stream.

As he charged forward, I slipped the ring onto my index finger and prepared to dash home. I didn't particularly want it, but I sure wasn't giving it to Buck Peterson.

Suddenly, I felt strange, kind of like I do when I get carsick. My stomach heaved over and I thought I might vomit.

Uh oh. What's happening?

I could see right through Buck Peterson.

Digging his heels into the dirt, Buck skidded to a stop. He went ghostly pale, and his eyes bugged out. He reached a shaky hand in my direction.

POOF!

Everything disappeared.

Chapter 3
Purple Prince

I rubbed my eyes.

Where am I? I asked myself.

I was dripping wet, but I wasn't in the park anymore.

Maybe I cracked my head open when I fell, I thought. *Maybe I'm in the hospital, delirious or dreaming. That's it! I'm dreaming.*

There was no other logical explanation.

Wherever I was, it was hotter than summer in—in heck. (I'm not allowed to say the other word.)

I pulled off Sam's jacket and felt cooler, right away. I folded it with the wet, bottom edge on the inside, and stuffed it into my backpack. I was wearing a red T-shirt under a striped, button-front shirt. I rolled up the long sleeves. I'd have been more comfortable if I took it off too, but there wasn't room for it in my backpack and I didn't want to carry it.

I glanced around.

I was in a room about the size of the basketball court at the high school. I had to tip my head way back to see the strange designs carved on the ceiling. Weird looking furniture, most of it bigger than a pickup truck, was scattered around. In the middle of the floor were five huge statues.

They were the oddest looking things I ever saw.

Each statue's skin had been painted a different color. One was pumpkin orange. One was sky blue. One was apple green. One was canary yellow. The last one was light purple. I couldn't think of a noun—like pumpkin or canary—to describe that shade of purple. I only know things like pumpkin orange and canary yellow because Brittney says stuff like that. She probably knows half a dozen words to describe light purple. All I know is that it wasn't plum purple, which is dark and not light.

Instead of hair, on top of the statues' heads were quills the same color as the skin, only darker. The light purple statue had plum purple quills. There was something different about the blue statue. It had something bulgy on the top of its head and quills hung down below it in the back. Maybe it was some kind of weird hat.

All of them had eyes shaped like eggs with the big end pointed toward their wide noses and the small end pointed at their long, droopy ears.

For clothes they wore shorts to their knees. Their shirts had round collars and square buttons. Their boots went just above the ankles and had silly turned-up toes. I couldn't see any stockings. Two of the statues were girls, I think, the blue one and the orange one. Their quills were quite long in the back, and their shorts were kind of puffy and had flowers on them. I don't know any boys who will wear clothes covered with flowers.

I crept behind the statues as quietly as I could. I didn't know who lived in this strange place, but I was sure I didn't want to meet them.

When I was real close, I realized I wasn't even as tall as the blue statue's knees, and it was the shortest. Reaching out, I stroked its leg to see how slippery it was. I thought I just might try climbing to the top of the head to check out the hat.

"Eeeeeiiiii," the statue screamed. "Something touched me!"

Gi-normous feet hopped from side to side.

"Yikes!" I screeched. I bolted to the left. A big blue foot crashed to the floor in front of me. I dashed to the right. The other foot slapped the ground behind me.

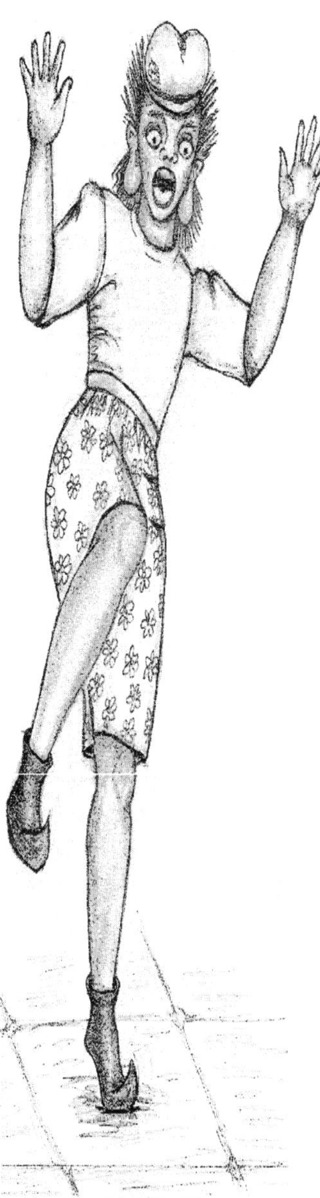

I ran.

"There it goes," a voice cried out.

I ran faster than I ever have before.

I ran and ran and ran.

I spied a piece of furniture that reminded me of Dad's recliner, but it had a dust ruffle around the bottom. Throwing myself to the floor, I slid on my stomach, just like a baseball player reaching for home plate.

Swoosh.

I was safe under the chair.

"I'll grab a broom," someone offered. It was probably one of the girls. Boys don't think about things like brooms. A boy would've said, "I'll go get a baseball bat or a fishing pole."

"No," a different voice said. "He's frightened enough already. We're lucky he wasn't squashed to death by Jenfer jumping and hopping all over the place."

"What is it?"

"A boy my father summoned. Now, go sit down. I'll explain in a minute."

"Yes, Prince Seth."

I pressed my back against a hind leg of the chair. *Now would be a good time to wake up.*

In front of me, the ruffle was lifted. A large purple face with pale blue eyes peered under it.

"I'm Prince Sethadorian. My father wanted to greet you, but he's sick and doesn't have the strength to get out of bed."

Come on, Timmy. Wake up. Wake up now!

"You're already awake," the prince said. "Welcome to Shalamar. Timmy? Is that your name?"

He can read my mind. Now I know I'm dreaming.

Big purple lips smiled around gleaming white teeth. "I can hear your thoughts. You're a very loud thinker. Will you please come out so we can talk?"

Dumb question, I thought. *I'm not budging until I wake up.*

"All right, we can talk where we are." Prince Seth took a deep breath. "It would be easier if you trusted me. When my father wants people to believe him, he pulls their minds into his so they can see the truth for themselves. My magic isn't that strong." A great sadness sounded in the giant's voice.

Curiously, I peered around the chair leg and looked at the prince. He had tears in his eyes.

Giants don't cry, I said to myself. *They're too big and strong. They can do anything they want. Why would they cry?*

"There are many things we can't do," said the prince. "If we could do everything, we wouldn't need you so badly."

"Need me?"

"Our world is in terrible trouble. That's why my father made the ring. He knew it would bring someone small enough to help us."

"Me? Help a giant?" I couldn't stop myself. I burst out laughing. "Puny little me help a giant?" I laughed some more.

"Ah," said the prince with a happy sigh. "The ring chose the right person. Only someone extremely brave can laugh at fear. You're the one we need."

Chapter 4

Terrible, Terrible Trouble

"No one will hurt you," Prince Seth said. "Please come out."

What else could I do? Even in a dream, I'd get bored if all I did was sit under a chair.

Besides, Prince Seth seemed like a nice guy. For one thing, he didn't make people try to say his whole name, Prince Setha—Sethoscope?—Sethamazoo?—Setha-something.

"Prince Sethadorian," he said.

"All right, Prince Seth," I said. "I'll come out, but scoot back."

The purple face disappeared.

I crept forward and cautiously lifted the edge of the ruffle. Prince Seth sat on the floor with his legs crossed. He was far enough away that I was out of arms reach.

"Don't move," I said. After I crawled from under the chair, I stood with my back pressed against it.

"You're just the right size," the prince said, studying me and then giving a nod. "You might be a little taller than the fish-wishers, but not by much." He cupped his hands and lowered them to the floor. "If you allow me, I'll carry you over to the table so you can meet my friends."

Those huge purple fingers could've crushed me like a soda can.

No, easier than that. They could've wadded me up like a piece of paper and tossed me into the nearest garbage bin.

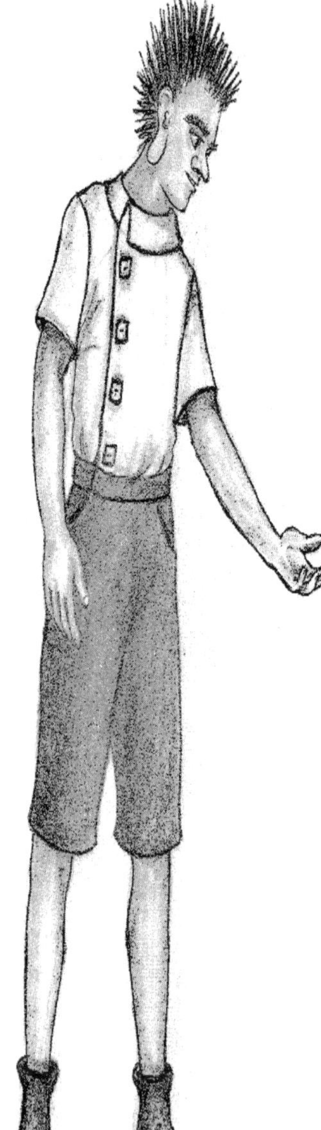

All of a sudden, staring at Prince Seth, I thought about the giant in "Jack and the Beanstalk."

"What a strange picture you have in your mind," Prince Seth said. "I promise you, no one here wants to grind your bones to make his bread." The prince made a disgusted face, and his shoulders quivered. "What a yucky thought, bread out of bones." He looked at me with a question in his eyes. "Do they really do that in your world?"

"Naw," I said, using the same tone Brittney had used with me when I asked her if vampires were real. "It's just a story, you know, make believe."

"I like stories," Seth said. "Perhaps before you go home you can tell me that story."

"Sure," I said. I felt a lot better since he mentioned I'd be going home. I felt safer.

"First though, I need to explain why you're here. May I carry you to the table?"

"Sure." I climbed into Seth's hands.

I wasn't afraid of him anymore. I began calming down when he got tears in his eyes and admitted there are things giants can't do. But when he said grinding bones for bread was "yucky," that did it. How can you be afraid of a guy who uses a word like "yucky?"

When we got to the table where the other four giants were sitting, Prince Seth pointed to a small chair that was centered on the table top. It looked as if it had been carved from a single piece of wood. It had a red cushion on the seat.

“Won’t you sit down?”

“Did your father make the chair,” I asked, running my hand over the back. The wood was very smooth and felt a little like microfiber, only stiffer.

“No,” Prince Seth answered. “I did. I made it a couple of years ago for my little sister’s doll house.”

“It’s great.” I dropped my backpack beside my feet, sat, and leaned back. The chair fit me exactly. “This is really comfortable.”

“Thank you.” The prince’s cheeks turned a darker purple, and he grinned at me. I was glad I wasn’t afraid anymore, because his teeth were really huge.

“Let me introduce you to the others,” Seth said. He pointed to the blue giant who’d almost trampled me. “This is Jenfer.” Now that I got a good look at her, I realized the odd thing on her head was definitely some kind of hat. It had a sparkly broach on the band.

“Next to Jenfer is Darrl.” He was yellow, and when he smiled he had dimples.

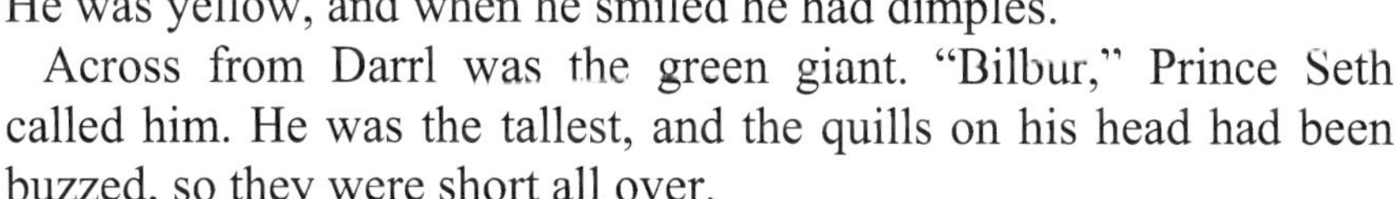

Across from Darrl was the green giant. “Bilbur,” Prince Seth called him. He was the tallest, and the quills on his head had been buzzed, so they were short all over.

“And this is Shandee,” Seth said. She was orange, and her mullet-style quills and dangling earrings reminded me of Brittney.

“Everyone, this is Timmy. He’s going to help us defeat Groklan by catching a fish-wisher for us.”

“I am?”

rse," Prince Seth said, bobbing his head up and down, s droopy ears wobble. "That's why the ring brought you

don't know what a Groklan is, or a fish-wisher."

"We'll tell you about them," Shandee said. She tossed her head and set her rusty orange quills rattling and her gold earrings swinging.

"Of course, we will," said Bilbur. He squinted and held his green hand above the table, just about the height I was while sitting in the chair. "Fish-wishers are little people, maybe this big."

"And—," Jenfer started to say something.

Darrl interrupted. "They're even smaller than you are."

"And—," said Jenfer.

Shandee cut her off. "They live in rocks over by the swamp. They're the only people the wish-fish will talk to."

"AND—," Jenfer shouted, jumping to her feet and glaring down at the others, "last week when my magic harp was singing, all of a sudden it stopped and said in order for us to defeat Groklan we had to find a fish-wisher. My harp can tell the future." She sat back down and added softly, "Sometimes."

Prince Seth smiled at her, and she grinned back at him. They reminded me of my brother Sam and his girlfriend, Grace. Lovey-dovey in the extreme. Eewww! Get a room!

It wasn't until the prince blushed dark purple that I remembered he could read my mind.

Sorry, I thought at him.

He cleared his throat. "Groklan is king of the g'nome g'nasties, and he is the reason we need a fish-wisher."

All of a sudden, I felt a wave of panic.

Wish-fish? Fish-wishers? G'nome g'nasties?

I'm not dreaming. I'm going crazy. I'm getting out of here.

Leaping up, I swept my eyes right and left.

"Wait," Prince Seth cried, "you're not going crazy. Give us a chance to explain."

I sat back down. Not because I wanted to listen, but because I realized I couldn't get off the table without help.

"In Shalamar," Seth said, standing up, "there are five different kinds of people. Tall ones like us are called k'nick k'nockers."

"Kick konckers?" I asked, trying to make the words sound

like something familiar.

"No!" all the giants said at once.

"KUH-nick KUH-nockers," Prince Seth said very clearly. "Next in size are the g'nome g'nasties. That's pronounced GUH-nome GUH-nasties." With his hand he marked a distance about halfway between his shoulder and elbow. "They're not very nice. And all of them are some shade of green."

"There's nothing wrong with green," Bilbur said, sounding a little angry. "I like green."

"But," said Shandee, "a whole race that is only one color?" She shivered. Her big earrings rattled against her dark orange quills. "That's just too weird."

"K'roll k'pollies are short and round." Seth held his hand near his knees. "They come to about here."

I guess I looked pretty vacant, because he repeated the name.

"KUH-roll KUH-pollies. It's kind of hard to know exactly how tall they are. They can pull their legs and arms into their bodies or stretch them out. It depends on if they want to roll or walk. Still, even when they stretch out, they're not very big."

"Except around the middle," Darrl snickered.

"I've already mentioned fish-wishers. They're about your size." Seth paused and looked at me, like he wanted to know if I remembered fish-wishers. So I nodded.

"The last race," he continued, "are the wish-fish. Actually, they might be the first. Their history goes back further than anyone else's. They have the strongest, wisest magic. They're very small and shy. All the races got along fairly well until Groklan crowned himself king of the g'nome g'nasties."

The other k'nick k'nockers began talking at once.

"Groklan is an evil magician," said Bilbur.

Shandee pointed to the window. "He's taken away the sun. Now it's dark and cloudy all the time."

"Since he stole the sun," Jenfer added, "no new baby k'nick k'nockers or k'roll k'pollies have been born. Maybe no babies of any kind."

Darrl's voice cut in. "And he steals people and makes them into slaves."

"Or," Bilbur added, "if he's in a bad mood, he feeds them to his pets."

"All the adults," Prince Seth said, "are sick and have lost their magic."

"I don't get it," I told them. "You said you guys are bigger than the g'nome g'nasties. Why don't you just go make Groklan give back the sunlight and free all the slaves? Then you could lock him up in jail or something."

Prince Seth and his friends fidgeted nervously.

"It's not that simple," said Seth. "You see, Groklan isn't like the other g'nome g'nasties. He is a . . . he's a giant!"

"Well, of course. You're all giants." Then I stopped and my mouth fell open. "You don't mean he's even bigger than you?"

Prince Seth nodded.

Dang!

Chapter 5
New Powers

A giant larger than Prince Seth? Taller than Bilbur? I tried to imagine it. The very idea scared me spitless.

"He's about so high." Seth stretched until his hand was up as far as it would go.

Darrl flung his arms out. "And about this wide."

"How big is your army?" I asked.

"There is no army," Prince Seth said. "There are only the palace guards, and they're sick like all the other adults."

Hmmm, that was the second time, or maybe the third, that Seth said the grownups were sick. I looked at each giant, trying to compare them to Brittney and her friends. "Say, how old are you guys, anyway?"

"Old enough!" Seth snapped in an angry voice.

"Oooops, I'm sorry," I said quickly. "I didn't mean to be rude. In my world it's only little old ladies who don't want to talk about their ages."

Seth sighed. "I'm not mad at you, Timmy. My friends and I are among the oldest k'nick k'nockers still healthy. When we told our friends that we were going ahead with my father's plan to defeat Groklan, they laughed at us. We may be young, but we can make

Shalamar safe again."

"If we don't," Jenfer said with tears running down her blue cheeks, "our parents will die, and then us."

"All we need is a fish-wisher and a wish-fish," said Shandee. Once again she set her orange quills and gold earrings rattling with a little toss of her head.

"They'll help us when they understand," Bilbur said. "We just need the chance to explain what's going on."

"Most of the time, wish-fish stay hidden in the swamps," said Darrl. "They won't get involved in other people's problems very often. They're too shy."

Smiling as if he was really proud to have such good friends, Seth nodded. "To answer your question, Timmy, I'm fourteen years old. So are Jenfer and Shandee. Bilbur and Darrl are nearly sixteen."

They're barely teenagers, I thought, *about Sam's age.*

"Teenagers," repeated Seth. "I like the sound of that."

"Most adults call us teenies," Shandee said to Timmy. "Isn't that about the worst thing you've ever heard?"

"It makes us sound like we're still babies," said Darrl.

"From now on we'll call ourselves teenagers," Bilbur said, expanding his chest proudly. "It sounds dignified."

"All right," Prince Seth said, "but right now, Timmy needs dry clothing and some food."

"He's just about the size of one of my old dolls," Jenfer said, shoving back her chair. "I'll run home and get an outfit for him. A nice blue one, I think. It's the least I can do for almost stepping on him earlier."

"No, thank you," I said quickly. "I'm just about dry." Trying to think very quietly, I added to myself, *I'd rather be wet the rest of my life than wear doll clothes, especially shorts and boots with turned up toes.*

"It was kind of you to suggest it, Jenfer," Prince Seth said, giving me a wink, "but I don't think we can spare the time."

"Oh," she said, sounding disappointed. She sat back down.

"Well," Bilbur said, "it's my turn in the kitchen. I'll make Timmy a lunch." He took a few steps then turned back. He pointed a long green finger. "The object you took off your back and set by your feet, is it for carrying things?"

"My backpack? Yeah, it holds lots of stuff."

"May I take it with me? If something is small enough to fit inside, it should be small enough for you to eat."

"Sure." Before dropping the pack into Bilbur's hand, I pulled out Sam's jacket to make room. Then I decided I'd better take out my harmonica too. I didn't want it ruined by any giant-sized crumbs.

"As soon as Bilbur returns," Seth said, "I'll carry you to the swamp so you can—"

"Today? Right now?" I asked while butterflies flitted around in my stomach. "Shouldn't I go through some kind of training first? I don't know anything about your world."

Jenfer bounced up and ran over to a cabinet by the wall. She rustled through some papers and chose one. She took it to Seth, and he spread it on the tabletop. It was a map.

"In the west," the prince said, tracing an area with his finger, "is the land of the k'nick k'nockers. In the east is the land of the k'roll k'pollies. Between them is the swamp, where the wish-fish and fish-wishers live. Groklan's palace is in the south."

"What's in the north?" I asked out of curiosity.

"Hills and mountains," Seth said. "The g'nome g'nasties used to live there before they moved south. Now there are probably just animals left."

"Dangerous ones?" I asked.

"There aren't many dangers in Shalamar," Darrl said, his yellow face looking serious. "Except the g'nome g'nasties."

"And the g'slith g'slythe," Jenfer said. "It likes to hunt in the rocks around the swamp. It's very dangerous."

"So are quird-birds," Shandee whispered, as if she was afraid one might hear and come after her.

"G'slith-g'slythe? Quird-birds? What are they?"

"Groklan's servants," Darrl said. "Quird-birds are big and ugly with gray feathers, brown spots, and dark red beaks. They can breathe poison or sleeping gas on you, depending on if they want to kill you or capture you."

The butterflies in my stomach turned into dive-bombers.

"The quird-birds," Prince Seth said, "are just dumb creatures that Groklan has trained to follow his orders. The g'slith g'slythe is different. My father thinks Groklan used magic to create it. It's a snake with two heads and two tails."

"If you come across it," Jenfer told me, "don't look into its eyes.

That's where it carries its magic, and it can paralyze you with its stare."

"Don't listen to it either," Darrl said. "Not only is it a liar, but its voice can—"

"It talks?" I squealed.

"Yes," Seth said. "But usually it stays close to Groklan's palace, so maybe you won't bump into it."

"Unless Groklan forgets to feed it," Shandee pointed out. "When it's hungry, it heads for the swamp. It really likes wish-fish and fish-wishers."

Not good, I thought, *I'm about the size of a fish-wisher. What if I'm mistaken for one? I'd better try one more time to wake up.*

I pinched my arm hard. Ouch. It hurt.

I don't think I'm asleep.

"What am I supposed to do if I see quird-birds or the g'slith g'slythe?" I asked. "Can I outrun them? Are there places to hide?"

"No," Seth said, shaking his head. "But my father gave the ring two special powers to help you out. The first one, of course, you're using right now."

"What! I'm not using any powers."

"Really?" Prince Seth said. "How do you explain being able to talk to us? I don't know what your native language is, but you've been speaking Shalamaran to us."

"Sounds like plain old American to me."

Nodding, Seth gently tapped the ring on my finger. "As long as you wear the ring, you can understand and speak any language. It can also take you places. All you have to do is think about the direction you want to go—up, down, right, left, forward, backward."

This could be fun. I sent my eyes around the room. *Where should I go first?*

"Slow down," Seth said. "It isn't as easy as you might think. You have to be very careful. The ring can only go in a straight line. It takes practice to learn how to maneuver around objects. Also, the louder you think, the faster the ring obeys and the faster you move. You're a very loud thinker. You'll need to—"

I stopped listening.

How can a person think loud? Thinking doesn't make any noise at all.

Grinning, I looked down at the ring.

Take me—
WHACK! I hit the ceiling.
—up.

Chapter 6

Monster in the Marshes

Absolutely terrified, I floated at the top of the room.

I was so high it made me dizzy. For a moment I was afraid I'd barf all over and embarrass myself.

I managed to hold it in by thinking about my predicament.

How do I get down without killing myself?

"Think quietly," Prince Seth yelled up at me.

Take me down, I tried to whisper mentally.

Too fast.

STOP!

I stopped so suddenly I just about got whiplash.

I bobbed in the air halfway between the ceiling and the floor.

Slowly, I thought as quietly as I could. *Down slowly.*

Thump!

I hit the table like a belly-flop in the swimming pool.

All the air swooshed out of my lungs.

"As with all magic," Seth told me, "you have to practice to get good at it. Be patient."

"If I don't kill myself," I grumbled.

Chuckling, he said, "That's a big *if.*"

Just then, Bilbur walked in holding my backpack by the straps. I was still flat on the tabletop, and I lifted my head a little so I could watch him. My backpack, held by those enormous green fingers, looked tiny. But when Bilbur put it down on the table beside me, it returned to its normal appearance.

"I hope you like your lunch. It was hard to decide what to fix for someone your size."

I hadn't quite caught my breath yet, and when I said "Thank you," it came out as a soft mumble.

I pushed myself to my knees, grabbed hold of my backpack, and then stood up shakily.

I re-rolled Sam's coat into a tight sausage-like bundle. Then I hooked it through the elastic loops on the bottom of my pack, the ones that can hold a liter bottle of pop. I poked my arms through the straps.

"Are you ready?" Seth asked.

I shook my head. "You haven't told me how I'm supposed to catch a fish-wisher if I find one."

"Just grab and squeeze him," Shandee said.

"No, no," Jenfer shook her head. "You ask them a riddle. If they haven't heard it before, they'll get you a wish."

"You're both wrong," Bilbur said. "You have to flatter them and pay them outrageous compliments."

"Don't be silly," said Darrl with a big laugh. "It's not that hard. Fish-wishers value politeness. If you're courteous—"

"As you can tell," Seth said, lifting me to his shoulder, "none of us knows for sure. We've never caught one so we don't know what works. You might just try explaining the situation."

I sighed.

"If I catch one, what do you want me to do with it?"

"Invite him to the palace. I'll handle the rest."

As Seth started walking, I grabbed onto his collar so I wouldn't slide off.

When he reached the door, the other giants called goodbye to me. I waved at them.

Outside, we cut across a big yard, weaving in and out of what passed for plants in Shalamar. I had a great view.

The grass was bluish-green, but the blades weren't straight and tapered. They were ruffled around the edges like lace. The trees had feathers instead of leaves and grew in pairs, twisting and turning around each other, making odd designs with their trunks.

Blue butterflies as big as bicycles fluttered around pink and orange striped flowers that were shaped like hearts. Tiny lavender hummingbirds hovered over sparkly blossoms that might have been made of glass, or maybe ice.

And the air!

Yummy.

It smelled like sugar cookies with just a hint of cinnamon.

In the distance I saw a herd of black and white cows grazing beside some reddish brown horses. I have never been on a farm and the only horse I've ever ridden was a pony at the State Fair, but it felt nice to see something that looked so normal—like home, like Earth.

Then suddenly, the cows and horses spread their wings and flew away.

I almost fainted.

Then I imagined how my dad would react if he saw a cow flying over his car, and I started to snicker. Dad won't park under trees or telephone wires because he's afraid the birds will make a mess on his shiny new, silver Beemer. A flying cow would probably give him a heart attack.

Even stranger than flying cows, though, was the quiet.

No birds sang.

No dogs barked.

No bees buzzed.

There was no whistling wind or gurgling water.

The only sound was the soft thudding of Prince Seth's feet.

"This is as far as I can take you," Seth said after quite a trek. "Fish-wishers hide when k'nick k'nockers get too close. Unless we're on our flying carpets, they're afraid we'll step on them."

"Flying carpets? If you have flying carpets, why did you walk here?"

Very carefully Seth lifted me from his shoulder.

"You have to be sixteen to get your flier's license. My father lets me practice around the palace sometimes, but he always starts the carpet for me. He won't give me the password until I take the test and have my license."

"My brother, Sam, is in a similar situation," I said, thinking about how bad Sam wants his driver's license. "I guess parents are the same all over."

"I suppose so." Pointing to some bulrushes, Seth changed the subject. "That's the beginning of the swamp. A little further down are the rocks the fish-wishers live in. You'd better wait here until I leave. Good luck."

"Don't go," I cried. "I have more questions."

But Prince Seth had already taken several steps away, and with his gigantic stride, I wasn't even sure he heard me.

I was all alone in a strange land.

Miserably I plopped down beneath two twisty trees that could've been an advertisement for Sprite. One was lemon yellow, both the trunk and the feathery leaves, and the other was lime green. I wished I hadn't thought about Sprite. I was thirsty and a soda would've tasted really good right then.

Thinking about a soda made me think about home. Thinking about home made me think about Mom. Thinking about Mom made me worry about what she was going to do when I didn't came home from school today.

I knew I wasn't going to make it home by bedtime. When supper was ready, my folks would start calling the neighbors. By dark, they'd call the police. If I died here, they'd never know what happened to me. Mom might even think I ran away because she made me wear Sam's jacket.

I have never felt more depressed.

Not knowing what else to do, I pulled my harmonica from my pocket and began playing softly. Music always makes me feel better, and I chose a bright, cheerful tune.

Skritch. Scratch.

What was that? I stopped playing and looked around.

Nothing.

Putting the harmonica to my mouth again, I blew a few notes.

Skritch. Scratch.

I jumped up. I knew I'd heard something that time. I looked all around, but I didn't see anything odd.

Odd? The whole darned place is odd, I thought.

Nothing but silence.

With my eyes still darting around, I leaned against a tree and began playing my harmonica again.

Skritch. Scratch. It sounded like it was right above my head.

Dang Prince Seth. He didn't tell me if the g'slith g'slythe can climb trees. Or where quird-birds live.

I waited and waited and waited.

Nothing happened.

Maybe it had just been the wind.

When everything had been still for several minutes, I gave up. I sat back down and started composing a Shalamar tune. I wanted to create sounds for the silent butterflies and flying cows, for the lacy grass, twisty trees, and crystalline flowers.

Skritch.

Scratch.

Plop.

A tiny white fuzz-ball dropped from the tree into my lap.

It had a miniature dog's head that stuck out of the fluff at one end and a wispy tail at the other. I didn't see any legs, but four paws seemed to be in the right places.

"Yip, yip, yip," it squeaked, wagging its whole rear half.

Using just one finger, I stroked its back. The little creature jumped in the air and did a somersault, landing on its back and spreading its paws as if it wanted me to scratch its belly. So I did.

"Yip, yip, yip," it barked contentedly.

It flipped over and nuzzled my hand. Then it jumped up and landed on my shoulder. After it turned around a few times, it lay down and started making a humming noise that sounded a lot like purring.

"I guess we're friends," I said. "Do you like music?"

I began playing again and it purred in rhythm with me. I figured that meant yes.

When I finished the tune, I put the harmonica away, hooked an arm through a strap of my backpack, and headed for the swamp.

"Since I don't know what you are, I'm going to call you Mozart. He's my mom's favorite composer."

Even though Mozart was only a little bigger than my fist, talking to him made me feel less alone.

"I'd better start looking for a fish-wisher. It's a long walk to the castle, and I want to get back before dark."

Rustle, crackle, crunch.

Reeds rippled and swayed.

There was no breeze.

"Is that one of them?" I whispered to Mozart. I wanted to rush forward and see. Still, something held me back. What if it wasn't a fish-wisher? What if it was something else?

"Fish-wisher?" I called softly. "Oh, fish-wisher?"

The bulrushes parted.

Peering at me were two bluish heads with red eyes. The heads were attached to a long body covered with scales in a green and yellow pattern of diamonds and triangles. At the end were two tails.

I stared.

"Yip, yip, yip." Mozart jumped up and down on my shoulder in a panic. "Yip, yip, yip."

"What isss it?" one head asked, flicking its black tongue in my direction.

"I'm not sssure," said the other.

"It isss the right sssize for a fish-wisher."

"But it isss not the right color."

The two headed snake slithered closer and closer.

"I know what it isss," the first head said.

"What?"

"Sssupper!"

Chapter 7
Knock, Knock

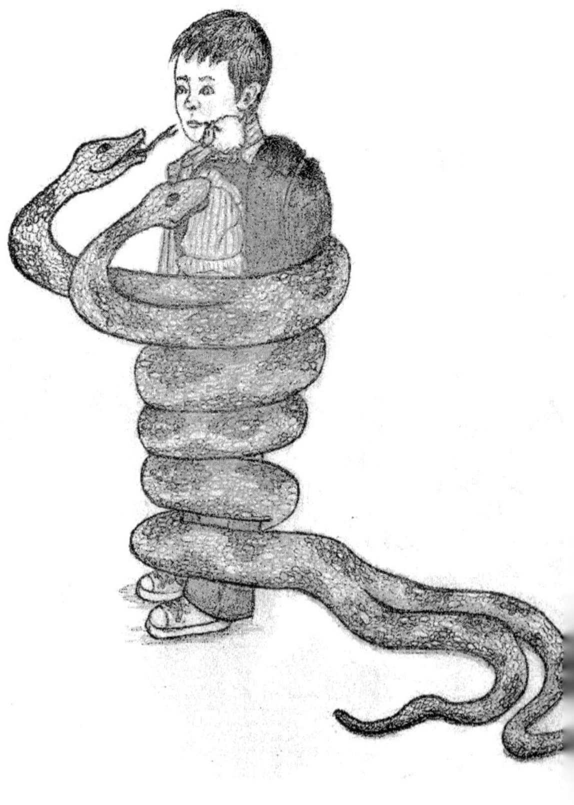

The g'slith g'slythe began to slowly wrap itself around my legs. It pulled its coils tighter and tighter.

Soon, I could hardly breathe.

Red eyes pinned me as if I was a bug stuck to a card in the Natural History Museum.

I couldn't move.

I couldn't look away.

I couldn't think.

"What isss that white thing?" one head asked.

"A sssnack?" the other said hopefully.

Two long black tongues flicked toward Mozart.

With a loud yip, he jumped onto my head.

"I'll get it," said the first head. "You must ssstare at thisss creature ssso it doesn't essscape."

"I'll ssstare if you'll ssshare."

The first head stretched its neck until its face was on a level with mine. As it talked, its tongue brushed against my nose. I would have thought it tickled if I hadn't been so terrified.

"It isss my sssnack. I sssaw it firssst."

"Ssshare or I won't ssstare."

"No. It isss too sssmall."

"Ssshare!"

As the snake argued with itself, I felt the coils loosen. I knew there was something I could do to escape, but I couldn't remember what.

If only the red eyes would look away.

Suddenly, one head swung around and batted the other.

"You ssselfish sssnake," it hissed.

The other head pulled back and whacked the first.

As soon as the two heads glanced away, I could think again.

Ring, I yelled in my mind. *Up.*

Zoom.

I shot skyward.

Halt!

With a teeth-rattling jerk, I stopped before going into orbit.

Poor little Mozart lost his footing, and his paws scrambled against my forehead for a toehold. Before he plunged to his death, I grabbed him and shoved him into my shirt pocket.

"Whew, that was close."

I looked down. Bad idea. The dizziness and nausea were even worse than when I slammed into the palace ceiling. This time Prince Seth wasn't there to talk me down.

"What do I do now?" I asked Mozart. He was trembling and peering up at me from my pocket. I petted him with my finger.

"Don't worry, I'll get us down."

Whiz.

Before I could blink, we zoomed toward the ground.

Slowly, I whispered in my head. *Very slowly.*

Like a feather falling on a windless day, we drifted lower and lower. When we were just above the trees by the swamp, I stopped and looked around.

I didn't see the g'slith g'slythe anywhere.

Scattered among the reeds were gray and brown rocks that looked a lot like Volkswagens with roundish holes in place of the windows and doors. Some of them were dotted with splashes of color as if they had been caught in the crossfire of a paintball game.

Forward, I thought quietly. *Right. Left.*

I zigzagged back and forth across the marsh until I was sure the two-headed snake was gone.

Down.

I stood with my hands on my hips, trying to decide what to do next. I saw a stick, a little longer than a baseball bat and just about the same shape. I used it to rap on the closest rock.

"It's polite to knock before going into someone's house," I told Mozart. "Besides, if the g'slith g'slythe is in there, I'm armed. I'll bash in its skull. Both skulls!"

No answer. I poked my head through an opening, but the inside was empty.

One after another, I thumped on rocks. Big ones. Small ones. Painted ones. Plain ones. Those on the edge of the marsh. Those farther in.

I splashed through puddles of standing water until my shoes and jeans were sopping wet again. I shouldered my way through a billion bulrushes.

No one was home anywhere.

Frustrated, I sat on a hillock and put the stick down next to me. I could spend the rest of my life wandering around the swamp knocking on rocks.

"What am I supposed to do now?" I grumbled.

I didn't want to spend all day in the swamp, and maybe all night too, but what else could I do? If I used the ring to go back to the palace, what would I tell Prince Seth? That I was a failure? That the ring hadn't chosen the right guy after all?

Dang it! I just want to go home and have dinner with Mom and Dad and Sam and Brittney.

Well, if I couldn't go home, at least I could have a meal. Bilbur made lunch for me.

Maybe after I ate something, I'd feel better.

I plopped my backpack down in front of me.

Movement in the rushes.

“What’s that?” I whispered.

Mozart poked his head out of my pocket but he didn’t yip.

Was that a good sign or a bad one?

I closed my fingers around the end of the stick.

The movement stopped.

As quietly as possible, I got to my feet. My eyes strained to see through the reeds. I took a step forward.

The plants swished.

Closer.

Closer.

Now right in front of me.

I raised the stick ready to swing.

WHAM!

Something smacked me from behind.

I tumbled forward, face in the dirt, while a heavy weight pinned me down.

A voice yelled triumphantly, “All right, fish-wisher, I’ve got you now. I want a wish.”

Chapter 8

Bumbling Brothers

Desperately I wriggled, trying to get free.

Something, or someone, sat on my back. My shirt had flopped open and I could feel Mozart pressed against my side, shivering. I was lucky I hadn't landed on him.

"Get off of me," I tried to shout, but it came out more like a grunt. I just couldn't get enough air in my lungs to yell.

Swish. Crackle. Snap.

Something else was rattling through the bulrushes.

The sound stopped.

"Uh, Niklus," a voice said. "I don't think that's a fish-wisher."

"Of course it is, Jonthun. No one else lives around here."

"But Gramma said fish-wishers are always green and blue, or yellow and orange, or red and black, or white and purple, or all one color. This thing doesn't match any of those."

I heard someone walking around me. I glimpsed dark blue boots with turned-up toes.

"I think maybe it's sick," the same voice said. "Look how pink it is. You'd better get off. Maybe it's contagious."

Suddenly the weight was gone.

I jumped up, ready to fight, but then my mouth dropped open in surprise.

In front of me were two beach balls with faces and hands and feet. One was about my height. The other was shorter. They were both brown, but different shades, and had blond fuzz for hair. The big one wore an outfit that was red on the right side of his shirt and orange on the left. His pants were just the opposite, red on the left and orange on the right. The short one's clothes were the same half-and-half pattern but in blue and purple.

"I still say it's a fish-wisher," said the larger one.

"I'm not," I told him. "My name's Timmy. I'm a human from planet Earth."

The k'roll k'pollies looked at each other a moment.

Then they started to laugh.

The big k'roll k'pollie put his fingers to his forehead like antennae and hopped around on one foot. "I'm Yagabban from the planet Millacoat."

"I'm a triboethean night bug," the little one said, flapping his arms like wings.

They chortled until they tipped over onto their sides.

"Earth! You'll have to do better than that, fish-wisher."

"Yeah," said the little one. "We're not dumb enough to believe in fairytales."

As they laughed harder and harder, they rolled around in circles.

No one likes to be laughed at, especially not by someone as ridiculous looking as a k'roll k'pollie.

I got angrier and angrier.

"I'm a human from Earth," I shouted. "Look at me. My hair. My clothes. My shoes. Do I look like someone from this stupid planet?"

The laughter died down. The k'roll k'pollies sat up with their feet stuck out in front and wiped their eyes.

"He has a point," said the small one. "He doesn't look very much like the drawings of fish-wishers in our history book."

"Well, whatever you are," the big one said, "my name is Niklus and this is my brother, Jonthun. If you're not a fish-wisher, what are you doing in the swamp?"

"I came to catch a fish-wisher."

Niklus bounced to his feet. "Not if we catch him first. We need a wish worse than you do."

"Actually," I said, "I don't need a wish at all. Prince Seth of the k'nick k'nockers does. His father made the magic ring that brought me here." I held out my hand so they could see the circle of gold on my finger.

"We still need a wish worse

than you," said Jonthun, bouncing up beside his brother. They glared at me in a threatening way.

Two against one. I didn't like the odds, but I figured I could even things out. I sidled to the right. I had dropped my stick when Niklus tackled me. Now I grabbed it up and held it like a baseball bat. If they rushed me, they'd be sorry. They were just too big to miss. *Ground ball past second base,* I thought as I pictured how far I could knock them.

They didn't come at me.

Instead, Jonthun got big tears in his eyes, and Niklus patted him on the arm.

"Yesterday," Jonthun said, sniffling, "the g'nome g'nasties raided our village. They built a fire around the outside so no one could roll away."

"And they had big nets," Niklus said, "so no one could bounce over the flames. They got everyone."

"Except us."

"I'm sorry," I told them, feeling a bit foolish. I lowered the stick. "How did you get away?"

Now Niklus got tears in his eyes too. "Our mom was going to bake us a wham-k'bam pie for dinner. We were in the forest picking berries."

"When we smelled smoke, we rolled right home."

"We got there just as our family was shoved into a wagon." Niklus wiped his cheeks with the back of his hand. "Then the g'nome g'nasties whipped the horses, and they all flew away."

"We've got to find a fish-wisher," Jonthun said, "so we can wish for our family—"

"—for the whole village—"

"—to come back again."

"Or," Niklus said, "we could just wish for all the g'nome g'nasties to disappear."

"But that's what the k'nick k'nockers want too," I told them.

"Are you going to hit us with that stick?" asked Niklus. "I don't like getting hit."

"Me either," said Jonthun.

They looked so nervous I tossed the stick away without another thought.

"Yip, yip, yip." Mozart poked his head out of my pocket, and I scratched him behind the ears.

"If you're not from Shalamar," Niklus asked in a suspicious voice, "what're you doing with a fuzzle-wuzzle?"

"A what?" I asked.

"A fuzzle-wuzzle." Niklus pointed to Mozart. "Don't act like you don't know what it is."

"I call him Mozart," I said. "He's my friend."

"You're a fish-wisher!" Niklus and Jonthun yelled together.

"You're trying to cheat us out of a wish," Niklus howled.

"Cheater. Cheater," Jonthun shouted.

Backing up, I shook my head. "I told you who I am."

"No one but fish-wishers have fuzzle-wuzzles for pets."

"You're such a liar," screamed Jonthun.

Dang. They tricked me into getting rid of the stick. I guess I can use the ring, but how will I ever catch a fish-wisher? First, the g'slith g'slythe. Now, the k'roll k'pollies.

"Listen, guys," I said, trying to reason with them, "I'm Timmy Parker from the planet Earth. I am not a fish-wisher."

"You can't fool us again," said Jonthun.

"We'll squeeze you until you promise to find a wish-fish for us." Niklus charged forward.

Left, I told the ring.

I zipped to the side.

Niklus rolled to a stop and glanced around. He yelled at his brother. "Get him."

Jonthun jumped, bounced twice, and grabbed at me.

Back.

"Stop it, you guys. Let's talk."

Niklus and Jonthun rushed me from opposite directions.

Up.

Crash! The brothers slammed into each other. Niklus flew one way. Jonthun flew the other.

Bounce, bounce. Jonthun hit a rock.

Bounce, bounce. Niklus hit a tree.

Whoosh! As if shot from two separate cannons, they ricocheted right back at me.

Snatch. Grab.

Niklus got my right leg. Jonthun got the left.

Higher.

The brothers let go, and I bobbed in the air above their heads.

Niklus pointed at me. "You can't hide up there. When I get you, I'll give you such a squeeze your eyes will pop out."

Niklus jumped a tiny hop, and landed on his bottom. Bounce, he went up.

It was so funny looking, I had to laugh.

This is stupid, I told myself. *I feel like I'm playing k'roll k'pollie dodge ball. I'll never get home this way.*

Bounce. Bounce. "Got you!" Niklus had his hands clasped around my ankles. We started to go down.

Forward. Back.

As the ring jerked me first one way then another, Niklus lost his hold. He dropped to the ground and bounced a couple of times before stopping beside his brother.

They scowled at me.

I drifted down, but I kept my distance from them once I landed.

"Hey, you two. I'm going to say this one more time. Listen carefully. I am a human boy named Timothy Alan Parker. I come from the planet Earth. I AM NOT A FISH-WISHER."

A soft giggle came from the swamp. "Of course you're not."

Chapter 9

Fish-Wisher

"Huh?" I spun around. "Who said that? How do you know what I am?"

"Well, I don't exactly know what you are," the voice said. "But I know you're not a fish-wisher, because I am."

The reeds swayed and a strange being stepped forward. Except for the face, hands, and feet, which were pale green, its body was covered with tiny blue scales. Fins poked out of the sides of the wrists and ankles. Its bright green hair stuck out in all directions like an untidy haystack. It wore black pantaloons with wide suspenders that met in a V at the waist.

"Yes," shrieked Niklus. Stretching out his arms—which could really stretch pretty long—he rushed forward. The fish-wisher jumped away.

Niklus screeched to a stop. He whipped around. "Wh-wh-where?"

"No grabbing and squeezing," the fish-wisher said, shaking a finger at the k'roll k'pollies. "I hardly ever ask wish-fish to help people who grab and squeeze me. You just keep your hands to yourself."

"Grrrrrr." Niklus took a couple of big bounces.

The fish-wisher stepped to the side, and Niklus missed and hit a rock instead. He bounced off and slammed into Jonthun. The two of them went rebounding in different directions. Up. Down. Up. Down. They looked like basketballs being dribbled by an invisible giant.

I shook my head and wondered if all k'roll k'pollies were a little dumb. Maybe so much bouncing around and hitting things scrambled their brains or something.

When the brothers rolled to a stop, the fish-wisher pointed at them. "Now, you two sit there and be still. If you don't, we'll never become friends, and I only get wishes for my friends. Do you understand?"

Niklus rocked from one foot to the other, back and forth, back and forth. He opened his mouth as if he wanted to say something. The fish-wisher frowned at him and pointed at the ground.

He shut his mouth and sat down.

"That's better." Then the fish-wisher studied me like the cover of a book it might want to buy. "I thought humans were only in fairytales, but you look solid enough. Are you really from Earth?"

"Yes. My name's Timmy."

The fish-wisher scowled at me and tapped its foot impatiently. I don't know what I did wrong, but it looked at me like I was a book that it wanted to toss into the fireplace and burn.

"I heard you tell the k'roll k'pollies that your name was Timothyalanparker. Don't you know your own name? Or were you lying?"

"I knew he was a liar," Jonthun said.

"I'm not a liar. My full name is Timothy Alan Parker, but on Earth people sometimes have nicknames. That's like a shorter name. My nickname is Timmy."

"Oh," the fish-wisher said, "that's all right then. My name is Tashee. I don't have a shorter name. Tashee is pretty short anyway. Did you notice that both our names start with T. That's a good sign. We're probably going to be good friends." Giving Niklus and Jonthun a dubious look, the fish-wisher tapped a long skinny finger on its mouth. "I don't know about the k'roll k'pollies."

"Are you a girl or a boy fish-wisher?" I asked before I thought.

"What a rude thing to say!" shouted Tashee with a stomp of her foot. "Do you always ask mean questions?" Turning around, she headed for the swamp. "We're not going to be friends after all. Now I don't get to help anyone gets wishes. Wish-fish won't come near a person if she's angry. How terrible. Meeting new people and not being able to get wishes granted! Boys are so ignorant."

"She's a girl, you ninny," Niklus said.

By that time I'd figured it out myself.

Niklus called out. "Tashee, please don't go away just because the human isn't very nice. Jonthun and I are sitting here being quiet, just like you said."

Tashee paused in the middle of a step, but didn't turn around.

"I'm sorry," I said, thinking fast. "On Earth we don't have any fish-wishers. In fact, we don't have anyone at all as pretty as you. I was caught off-guard."

Spinning around, the fish-wisher beamed a deep emerald green. "You think I'm pretty?"

"Sure," I said. "You're beautiful." Anytime Brittney is mad at me, I can get around her by complimenting her looks. Seemed to work fairly well with fish-wishers too. "I didn't mean to be rude. Please forgive me."

Okay, I admit I was making myself sick with all the schmoozing, but I couldn't afford to have Tashee leave. I'd spent all day looking for a fish-wisher, and if she left, I'd probably spend at least a day or two trying to find another one. Better to have a bird in the hand than two in a bush. (It sounds stupid, I know, but Mom always says it.)

"All right," Tashee said brightly, as if she'd never had a bad mood in her life. "Let's start over again. I like making new friends, and I hate to miss an opportunity. You can tell me all about yourselves," she swept her hand to include me and both k'roll k'pollies. "Then I'll decide whether or not I like you. If I do, I'll ask a wish-fish to give you each a wish."

Tashee sat down on the ground, so I did too.

"Now tell me about your magic," she said to me.

"I don't have any magic," I told her.

"Don't be silly. All people have magic. That's the difference between people and animals, isn't it?" The last bit was addressed to Niklus and Jonthun.

"Of course," the brothers answered together.

Hooking a thumb proudly at himself, Niklus said, "I can roll super fast and bounce super high. Also, if I touch someone, I can make them roll faster and bounce higher than they could before."

"And I can roll up anything," Jonthun said, "even walls and cliffs, and across the ceiling, too."

"See," said Tashee, "even k'roll k'pollies have magic." Quick as a bolt of lightning, she grabbed my backpack. "I guess things could be different on Earth. Maybe you carry your magic in here. I feel something strange." She dumped the contents onto the ground. Out tumbled the lunch Bilbur had packed, followed by everything else. "Mmmmm, plum-nuts cake! And sliced sea-bees."

"Are you hungry?" I asked. I was starving. "I think there's plenty."

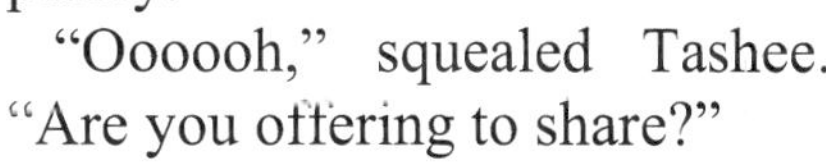

"Oooooh," squealed Tashee. "Are you offering to share?"

I nodded.

"That's very polite of you," she said.

"We have some wham-k'bam berries," Niklus said, bouncing to his feet. "We left our buckets behind the rock over there."

"Wonderful," Tashee cried, clapping her hands gleefully. "A picnic. We'll surely become friends now. But I have to share too. I'll be right back."

Swish. She ran through the reeds. Splash.

Niklus and Jonthun bounced away and came back with two small buckets with clip-on lids. They lifted the tops, showing me that each was half-full of bright yellow berries. A moment later, Tashee returned with four gray, lumpy, roundish things, a little bigger than a baseball. They were covered with patches of fuzz, like mold on a hunk of old cheese.

"Wow," exclaimed Niklus, "hair-pears."

"And one apiece," Jonthun added joyously.

Tashee gave me one first, and I shifted it from hand to hand. Was I supposed to peel it or just take a chomp? All of a sudden, it occurred to me that Shalamar food might be poisonous to humans.

"Go ahead," Tashee told me.

"Uhmmm, back on Earth, it's always ladies first."

"Really? How sweet." Tashee rubbed the fruit with her hand until the fuzz came off, then she took a bite. While she chewed, she tossed a fruit to each of the k'roll k'pollies.

After wiping the hair-pears on their shirts, they began wolfing them down. A delicious smell filled the air.

My stomach growled.

I decided I had to eat something. I might be here for days. I might as well find out if the local food was going to kill me.

I gave the gray lump a really good scrubbing on my jeans, and then I closed my eyes and took a nibble. *Holy cow!*

"It tastes just like peach ice cream," I cried. "That's my favorite."

Tashee grinned. "There are so many good things to eat in the swamp I wasn't sure which to choose. I'm glad Earth human boys like hair-pears. They're my favorite too."

As she ate, Tashee rummaged through my stuff. She picked up one of my pencils.

"What's this?"

"It's called a pencil."

"What's it for?"

"I'll show you." Using my arithmetic book as a table, I smoothed out a piece of wrinkled paper, picked up another pencil, wrote with it, and then erased the writing.

"Wow," Niklus said. He'd eaten his hair-pear and was munching on wham-k'bam berries while he watched. "We don't have anything like that in Shalamar. Maybe that's your magic."

"No," Tashee said thoughtfully, "it's a trick, not magic." She pointed to the rubber ball. "What's that?"

I got up and tossed the ball so it bounced on the ground before hitting a tree trunk. When it bounced back to me, I caught it.

"It's like a little k'roll k'pollie," Jonthun shouted. "Let me see." He and Niklus took turns throwing it down, watching it fly up, and then running after it when it bounced away. Their eyes bulged as if they couldn't figure out how it worked.

"That's not magic either," the fish-wisher said. She broke off a piece of plum-nuts cake and slipped it into her mouth.

The cake looked good, so I took a hunk too. It tasted a lot like the banana-nut bread with currants that my mom makes sometimes. The familiar flavor caused a wave of homesickness to hit me, and I could hardly swallow. I might have shed a few tears if Tashee hadn't jumped to her feet and glared at me.

"You have magic. I can feel it." She walked around me with her eyes squinted and her forehead all wrinkled. After a moment, she stopped, reached into my pocket, and pulled out my harmonica. "What's this?"

"It's a musical instrument," I told her.

"Mu-si-cal? What's that?"

"I'll show you." I took the harmonica from her and blew a few measures of *Here Comes Santa Claus* because it was the first thing that popped into my head.

The k'roll k'pollies let the rubber ball roll away. They turned slowly toward the music as if pulled on a string.

With her mouth open and her eyes big and round, Tashee stared at me in astonishment.

Time froze.

Silence held its breath.

After an eternity, Tashee spoke in a whisper I almost couldn't hear. "That's your magic."

Chapter 10
Which Wish

"It's not magic," I said. "It's music."

Making her hair swirl like tall grass in the wind, Tashee shook her head. "Call it what you want. It's magic. I feel it here." She clasped both hands over her heart. "Do it again."

Sitting on the ground, I played a little something I'd written. It was quick and lively, like those Irish tunes where people are tap-dancing so fast you can barely see their feet.

"Yip, yip, yip."

Mozart climbed out of my pocket and jumped onto my shoulder. He began to purr loudly.

"A fuzzle-wuzzle?" Tashee said, clapping her hands. "That proves it."

"Proves what?" I shoved the harmonica back into my jeans pocket so I could scratch Mozart's tiny head. The purring increased until he sounded like our lawnmower on Saturday morning.

"It proves your music is magic."

Mozart nuzzled my neck like a kitten, and then he hopped down and scampered over to Tashee.

"Most people think fuzzle-wuzzles like us fish-wishers because we're both so little. But they're wrong." Tashee lifted Mozart up and rubbed his fluffy fur with her nose. He licked her cheek, and his purring grew until it was like a motorcycle going into hyper-drive. "They're attracted to the magic we pick up from the wish-fish."

Niklus was eating another wham-k'bam berry. He stopped chewing. "People can't pick up each other's magic."

"Maybe I didn't say it right." Tashee tapped her fingers on her forehead, obviously thinking hard. "If you play in the dirt, what happens?"

"Mom makes him take a bath," Jonthun said, laughing.

"Why?" Tashee asked.

"Because you can't play in the dirt without getting dirty," Jonthun answered.

"Right. That's what happens to us. While the wish-fish swim around, they fill the swamp with magic. Then when we go swimming, it sticks to us like dirt does to you."

"Wow," Niklus said, rolling to his feet. "If I sit in the swamp, will I get more magic?"

"Sure, if you stay in long enough."

Up. Down. Up. Down. Niklus bounced with excitement. "How long?" he asked.

As he dribbled himself faster and faster, Tashee giggled. "Only a few years. Maybe ten or fifteen. Want to try?"

Thump. Niklus sat down with his lower lip stuck out. "No way," he said, frowning.

"Of course not," Jonthun said, laughing so hard he started to roll away. "It would be like a fifteen-year-long bath. He hates baths."

Tashee shrugged and took a slice of sea-bees and put it on top of a chunk of plum-nuts cake. Opening wide, she took an enormous bite. After she finished, she said, “Tell me about your wishes. I hope they’re exciting. I hate the boring ones.”

She fed a cake crumb to Mozart, and he happily wagged his rear end for her.

“Our family, our whole village, was taken away by the g’nome g’nasties,” Niklus said.

“We want them back,” said Jonthun.

“Oh, dear.” Tashee leaped to her feet and began pacing around in a circle. Mozart started to whine, so I picked him up and put him back in my shirt pocket. I crumbled up some cake and dropped it in with him. He yipped his thanks.

“Oh dear, oh dear, oh dear,” Tashee muttered. She stopped and looked at me. “Please don’t tell me you want a wish against the g’nome g’nasties too. It’ll ruin my whole day, my complete and total day.”

“Actually, it’s Prince Seth of the k’nick k’nockers who wants the wish. But, yeah, it’s about Groklan.”

“Oh, dear.” She changed directions and began walking in circles again, counterclockwise. Around and around and around she went, until I was getting dizzy watching her.

“What’s wrong with wishing against the g’nome g’nasties?” I asked her.

“What’s wrong?” Tashee repeated. “I’ll tell you what’s wrong. When the wish-fish council first found out Groklan was kidnapping people and had hidden the sun, they decided to get rid of him. With him gone, they could have made the rest of the g’nome g’nasties behave.

“His Majesty All-White Paterick, The High Fin, chose Red-Striped Floyd to make the wish. So Red-Striped Floyd wished that Groklan would turn into a mosquito and get eaten by a bog-frog.”

Tashee snapped her fingers. “Just like that, Red-Striped Floyd turned into a mosquito, and a bog-frog hopped by and ate him.”

“No,” gasped Niklus and Jonthun. “Impossible.”

“It frightened all the wish-fish so bad they swam to the bottom of the swamp and wouldn’t come up for a week.”

“What happened?” I asked. “Did the wish-fish make a mistake?”

“Wish-fish don’t make mistakes,” Niklus said.

“Never ever,” agreed Jonthun.

"Never before, anyway." Tashee studied the scales on her arm then ran her hand over them as if smoothing them down. "A few members of the council thought it was possible, though unlikely, that Red-Striped Floyd made a miscalculation. They decided to test the idea.

"His Majesty Paterick asked Black-Plaid Mary to make a wish that couldn't hurt anyone if it went wrong. She wished that all the male g'nome g'nasties would turn into tadpoles, appear in a big glass jar, and then become themselves again in one minute."

Tashee paused, and the k'roll k'pollies and I leaned forward anxiously.

"And?" I prompted.

"Poof." Tashee waved her arms in the air. "That's exactly what happened to all the male wish-fish, including the High Fin. When they turned back into themselves, they swam to the bottom of the swamp and wouldn't come up for a month. His Majesty Paterick is afraid to try again."

"We need to tell Prince Seth," I said. Grabbing my things, I shoved them into my backpack. I couldn't see the rubber ball, and decided to forget it, but Jonthun found it for me.

"Will you come with me, Tashee? And you, too, Niklus and Jonthun? Prince Seth needs to know what's going on. Maybe he'll have some ideas about what to do."

"All right, but we'd better hurry," Tashee said. "It's getting late and it's a long walk."

“We can bounce,” said Niklus. “It’s faster.”

“Would you carry my pack?” I asked him. “Tashee can ride on my back, and I’ll use the magic ring so we can keep up with you.”

“A magic ring?” said Tashee. “I’ve never traveled by magic ring before.”

“Do you have room in there for the wham-k’bam berries?” Niklus asked. “I hate to leave our buckets behind.”

“I think so.” I rearrange things to make room for the pails and then gave the pack to him.

Jonthun helped Tashee climb up on me, piggyback.

When the k’roll k’pollies bounced forward, I had the ring lift us a few feet off the ground. We glided through the air along side of them.

We didn’t really rush, but I felt we were making good time.

I gazed around, enjoying the scenery as much as I had when Prince Seth carried me to the swamp. Every direction seemed to have something new and strange to look at.

“What’s that?” I asked, pointing at a trail in the sky. “Is that yellow smoke, or is it some kind of cloud?”

“Oh no!” screeched Tashee. “Go faster, Timmy. Go faster. Hurry. Hurry. Hurry.”

“What is it?” I asked again.

The k’roll k’pollie brothers yelled the answer at the same time, “Quird-birds.”

Chapter 11
On the Run

The yellow streamers of smoke got closer.
"Bounce faster!" I cried.
The k'roll k'pollies stopped bouncing and started rolling.
Zip! Niklus took the lead, rolling head first with my backpack clutched to his chest.
Zap! I urged the ring to catch up.
We zoomed over a little hill covered with tall grass.
"Where's Jonthun?" Tashee shouted right in my ear.
Slowing down, I glanced over my shoulder.
Jonthun was way behind. Any minute now, the quird-birds would have him.
"I need to help Jonthun speed up," Niklus called as he flipped a U-turn.
When Niklus reached Jonthun, he touched him with a fingertip. As he pulled his hand away, a tiny bolt of electricity flickered between them.
Whoosh. Jonthun took off.
Whish. Niklus was right beside him.
Wham. I joined them.
The k'roll k'pollies hurtled around trees, skimmed over stones,

and flattened a path through flowers and grass.

Like a jet plane, I streaked through the air next to them.

"They're getting closer," shrieked Tashee. She pounded wildly on my shoulders. It startled me so much I almost crashed. "Hurry, hurry."

With a glance behind, I saw two gray blurs trailing yellow smoke. If they were the quird-birds, I thought, they were traveling at supersonic speeds.

They were going to catch us.

I think the ring can go faster than this, I told myself. *But Niklus and Jonthun seem to be at their top speed already. I wonder if I can lift them.*

Dropping down, I grabbed Niklus's shirt with my right hand and Jonthun's with my left.

"Hey," shouted Niklus, twisting so I nearly dropped him.

"Hold still," I yelled. "I'm going to try to carry you."

Faster, ring. Faster.

Zip. Whiz. Zoom.

The wind pulled at the k'roll k'pollies, making it hard for me to hold on to them.

I tightened my fists.

The brothers seemed to be getting heavier and heavier every second.

I didn't know how much longer I could maintain my grip.

"We're getting away," Tashee cried out. "The quird-birds are falling behind."

Ahead in the distance, I could see Prince Seth's palace. Maybe the quird-birds wouldn't follow us all the way there. Even if they did, the k'nick k'nockers probably had ways of dealing with them.

We were going to make it!

At that precise moment, I realized my fingers were going numb. The shirts of the k'roll k'pollies started to slip away. I was concentrating so completely on not letting go that I misjudged the distance to a tree.

I jerked aside at the last minute.

Niklus slammed into Jonthun, and I lost them.

Whappity, whappity, whap. They bounced away.

Slow down, ring. Turn around.

I tried to catch Niklus.

I reached down just as he bounced up. He smacked me in the stomach. In a jumble of arms and legs, we hit the ground.

Niklus ricocheted away.

Tashee flew off my back.

I somersaulted into a log, banging my head and scraping my arms.

Sprawled with my legs over the log and my head in the dirt, I tried to catch my breath. Every inch of me ached. Moving slowly, painfully, I rolled onto my side and sat up.

"Is everyone—?"

A few feet away, Tashee stared upward, transfixcd.

I followed her gaze. Two gray birds with brown spots and brick red beaks were directly overhead. From their nostrils, they blew yellow smoke at us.

"Come on, Tashee," I shrieked as panic seized me. I ran to her and grabbed her hand, but she didn't move.

Yellow mist drifted over her, and she toppled forward.

Holding my breath, I picked her up and ran. We could still make it to the palace.

My pace slowed.

Bright spots danced before my eyes. I needed to breathe, but I didn't dare. I staggered a few more steps then stumbled.

Falling to my knees, I hit with a jolt.

My mouth popped open and I took a deep gulping breath. It turned into a yawn.

No. Not when we're so close.

I yawned again.

I fought to keep my eyes open, to move out of the smoke.

My eyelids grew heavy.

Very, very heavy.

I let them fall shut.

Chapter 12

Danger in the Dungeon

Shivering, I woke on a hard, cold surface.

Had I fallen asleep on the floor in front of the television again? Must have. Boy, what a weird dream I had.

With an enormous yawn that almost dislocated my jaw, I stretched and squirmed until I worked myself into a sitting position.

"I'm glad you decided to wake up, Timmy. I think the k'roll k'pollies are going to sleep forever."

"Tashee!"

It wasn't a dream. It was real.

"Were you expecting someone else?" she asked. "I can't blame you if you were. I'm a little surprised that we haven't had any visitors yet."

"Where are we?"

"A dungeon. I've never been in one before, but this is exactly as I've always pictured them. I imagine we're Groklan's prisoners."

A big metal door with a barred window in it was centered on the front wall. Along the back was a trough with a thin stream of water gurgling down the middle. A wooden bench was pressed up against the wall on the right. The left side of the room was bare except for a hole in the floor. It had an unpleasant odor oozing from it.

Tashee walked over to the water trough and dangled her fingers in it for a second. "The water's clean enough for drinking if you're thirsty. And I'll turn my head if you need to—well, you know." Her cheeks went deep, deep green as she pointed to the hole.

I'm sure I blushed, but I needed to go, so I thanked her for her consideration. I glanced over my shoulder to make sure she was looking the other way, and then did what I needed to. When I was done, I washed my hands as well as I could without soap. Then I waited a moment, cupped my fingers, and took a drink.

"I'm hungry," said Tashee. "There's still food in your bag, isn't there?"

"If Niklus didn't lose it when he fell."

Niklus was lying with his back to me. I circled around him to look. He was clutching my backpack in his arms. Gently I lifted it away. I was pulling out smashed chunks of plum-nuts cake, when Niklus rolled over, sniffing.

"Breakfast?" he asked.

"About time," Jonthun said with a big yawn.

I got out their buckets of wham-k'bam berries and the last slices of sea-bees.

"Mmmmm, everything tastes so good," Tashee said as soon as she'd had a few bites. "I like to eat. It's ever so much more pleasant than being eaten, don't you think? I hope Groklan doesn't feed us to his pets. The g'slith g'slythe is very fond of fish-wishers, you know."

"You sure know how to ruin someone's appetite," Niklus said, setting down a handful of berries.

"Not mine," Jonthun said. He scooped up the berries and shoved them into his mouth.

"There's got to be a way to escape," I said. "There's always a way to escape."

Using the ring, I lifted up so I could see out the window in the top part of the door. It was covered with a grill, and I poked my head between the crisscrossed bars. I wriggled around, trying to squeeze through, but I couldn't. Maybe Tashee was narrow enough, but then what? It was a long way down to the floor, and she couldn't fly.

Maybe the keyhole was bigger. I checked. Nope.

I drifted to the floor and sat with my new friends. "I wonder if the door is even locked."

"What does it matter?" asked Niklus. "Look at how big it is. We couldn't open it anyway."

"If it was unlocked, we could try. Look," I pointed at the seam between the door and the wall. "There aren't any hinges in here. That means the door swings out. If we all pushed together we might get it to open far enough that we can squeeze through."

"Locked doors aren't a problem," said Tashee. "With my magic I can understand how mechanical things work. And I can move the parts around. The lock hasn't been created that I can't unfasten. But what's the use? Like the k'roll k'pollie said, the door is too heavy for us."

"But you can unlock it?" I asked.

"Sure." Tashee lingered over her last bite of plum-nuts cake, and then brushed her hands off on her bloomers. "Of course, you'll have to take me there."

She climbed on my back, and up we went.

Leaning forward, Tashee felt around the keyhole with her fingers. She stuck her whole arm in the lock, and pressed her ear against the outside.

Clink. Clank. Clunk.

"Oooooh," Tashee growled. "This is a tough one."

She pulled her arm out and smacked the lock a couple of times, then shoved her arm back in.

Jingle. Jangle. Jingle.

"Whew!" she said.

"You got it?"

"Not quite. The door's unlocked, but it's not unlatched. There's a handle on the other side that has to be turned."

"Dang!"

"I can cast a spell to turn the handle, but you'll have to be quiet and hold real still. Spells are tricky, and I don't use them very often." Cupping her hands around her lips, Tashee whispered into the keyhole.

Snick.

"Now," Tashee said proudly, "it's unlocked and unlatched."

"Good job. Let's get out of here."

We all lined up, shoulders pressed against the bottom of the door.

"On the count of three," I said. "One. Two. Three."

Heave-ho.

The door didn't budge.

"Again," I said.

I shoved my shoulder against the metal. Tashee turned around so she pressed with her back. Niklus and Jonthun used the flat of their hands. Even Mozart climbed out of my pocket and butted the door with his head.

Thrust. Strain. Grunt. Groan.

Not even a millimeter of movement.

"Let's all run and slam into it," Niklus suggested. "Maybe we can jar it open a crack."

"Might as well try," I agreed downheartedly.

We backed up all the way to the water trough to get a good running start. We lined up in a row. Niklus, then me, then Jonthun, and then Tashee.

"Ready. Set. Go," shouted Niklus.

We ran forward.

Wham! We hit the door.

Suddenly the room was full of ricocheting k'roll k'pollies.

They shot from wall to wall as if they were ping pong balls being hit back and forth by experts. I dropped to the floor and protected my head with my arms. Tashee did the same thing. Mozart ran around in circles, yipping loudly until he burrowed under me and squirmed into my pocket.

Even after the k'roll k'pollies wound down to a stop, I could feel the floor vibrate with their bouncing.

The ground shook.

Uh oh.

Something big and heavy was coming our way.

When I glanced at Tashee, she was staring at me. So were Niklus and Jonthun.

Not saying anything, Tashee pointed at the door and then climbed onto my back. I used the ring to lift us. Niklus gave an enormous bounce and Jonthun rolled right up the door. We all peered through the window.

Two giants were coming toward us.

A small one and a large one.

No, I thought, large was the wrong word.

Mammoth. Colossal. Gargantuan. Humongous.

He was scum-pond green with mustard yellow hair and beard. His arms and legs, rippling with muscles, were bigger than tree trunks. His head perched on a massive neck covered with protruding veins, and below that was a mountain range of shoulders. His ears were pointed like a devil. His lips curled in an evil sneer, showing sharp, pointed teeth. The eyes were glow-in-the-dark red.

He was the giant-est giant imaginable.

No one needed to tell me who he was.

Chapter 13
Nasty G'nasties

"Hide!" screeched Niklus.

Hide? I thought as I lowered myself and Tashee to the floor. *Where? The room's empty except for the bench and the water trough.*

Water trough!

Water flowed into the room through a hole in one wall and disappeared through another. Maybe we could slip out one of the openings.

Heavy footsteps thundered closer.

Gotta do something. Fast. I poked my head into the hole where the water emptied. *Dang. Bars.* I ran to the other end of the trough. *Double dang! Bars here too.*

My eyes darted around. No windows. No cracks in the walls. No other door. No escape.

Niklus rolled under the bench and pressed himself into the corner farthest from the door. Jonthun tried to squeeze behind him.

"Get your own corner," Niklus said, giving Jonthun a swat.

Jonthun rolled the length of the room. When he reached the wall, he gave it a kick.

Boing.

He shot straight back at Niklus, grabbed his arm, spun him around twice then let go. Niklus whirled away like a top. When he smacked into the door, he launched himself straight back at his brother. Soon they were rolling and bouncing all over each other.

"Quit it, you guys," I said. "We've got to stick together."

They didn't listen.

They had hold of each other's hands with their arms stretched way out and were slamming bellies and springing back as if they were playing paddleball with each other.

Niklus knocked Jonthun into my backpack and scattered the leftover food, my papers, pencils, and other stuff all around the room. Jonthun rebounded and smashed into Niklus, who would have bowled Tashee over if she hadn't jumped out of the way.

We tried to grab them and pull them apart.

I got hold of Niklus's foot.

Bounce. He was free.

Tashee grabbed Jonthun's shirt.

Twist. Roll. Jonthun got away, zipped up the wall and across the ceiling, then dropped and began jumping on top of Niklus.

Too angry to think of anything else to do, I grabbed up my things and shoved them into my backpack. My homework was completely ruined. Not that it would matter if I never got home again.

Creak. Scrape. Rasp.

The k'roll k'pollies froze like statues.

Tashee grabbed my arm with both her hands.

Mozart poked his head out of my pocket.

The door moved.

Quick as a wink, we all dashed under the bench and crowded together. Jonthun sucked in his round belly, trying to make himself smaller. He held his breath with his cheeks puffed out until his face turned dark brown, almost black.

Niklus pounded him on the back. "Breathe, Jonthun, or you'll pass out. That won't help."

Gasp! Jonthun gulped in a deep breath.

Light poured into the room, and then two shadows blended together and blotted it out again.

"Get a broom," a deep voice commanded.

Footsteps scurried away.

Jonthun started to sniffle. "What are we going to do?"

As if they'd never fought in their lives, Niklus put his arms around his brother. "Don't cry. Timmy'll think of something."

"Me?" I gagged on my tongue and went into a coughing fit.

"Of course, you," said Tashee. "You're the one the ring chose. It's your job to take care of us. That's why you have such powerful magic."

"It's music not magic," I hissed at her. "Remember? I don't have any magic."

"Says you," Tashee told me in a haughty tone. "You just have to figure out how to use it."

"I would if—" My sentence was interrupted by a new sound.

Thunk.

Something hit the floor.

A shoebox-like object made of steel mesh was scooted under the bench. A door was propped open at one end.

A cage.

Swish. Swipe. Sweep.

Someone swung a broom at us.

We darted one way. The broom was right behind us.

We jumped. There it was

again.

Run to the right. Broom.

Dash left. Nowhere to go except—

Whish. The broom swatted us into the cage. Niklus and Jonthun rolled all the way to the back. Tashee and I tumbled in right behind them.

Bang. The door closed.

Snick. A lock clicked shut.

"Got you!"

Green hands with long knobby fingers reached under the bench and pulled out the cage. It was lifted until it was even with pale yellow eyes. A grinning green mouth exposed pointed teeth, brown with decay. It was the small giant.

Small giant. Right!

"Ugly little beasties, aren't they?" the g'nome g'nasty said.

He raised the cage higher so the huge figure in the doorway could see us.

"I didn't give you permission to speak," the larger giant grumbled. "Speak out of turn again, Ugor, and I'll slice and dice you and feed you to the quird-birds."

"Yes, Master," Ugor said. Then he clamped a hand over his mouth and quaked.

Glow-in-the-dark red eyes glared at him a moment. Then he switched the gaze to us.

Groklan was as terrifyingly hypnotic as the g'slith g'slythe.

He turned away and tromped down the hall. "Bring them."

Chapter 14

Tall and Short Giants

Motion sickness has been a curse my whole life. I get carsick, seasick, airsick, and elevator-sick. If the dentist isn't careful and makes me go up or down too fast, I even get dentist-chair-sick.

So of course Ugor swung the cage back and forth, back and forth, as he walked. Sooner or later I was going to throw up. I knelt with my face pressed against the mesh, so I wouldn't get vomit all over my friends.

As Ugor followed Groklan up a flight of stairs, he tipped the cage at an angle and hooked it under his arm.

Tashee slid across the bottom and rammed into me.

Hoomph! My breath whooshed out, and I almost lost my breakfast then and there.

Whump. Niklus and Jonthun rolled into Tashee.

They all piled up on top of me. Niklus's elbow jabbed me in the ribs. Jonthun's foot caught my knee. Tashee's head was pressed against my chest with her spiky hair prickling my nose.

"Ah-ah-ah-choo!" I sneezed then rubbed my face and swallowed hard several times.

Ugor switched the cage to his other side. I hooked an arm through the mesh, closed my eyes, and groaned.

Whish! There went Tashee and the k'roll k'pollies.

Blam. They smacked into the mesh opposite me.

With my free hand I checked on Mozart. The poor little thing was scrunched down in my pocket, trembling with fear. I stroked his fuzzy fur with my fingertip.

Ugor shifted the cage again.

Oh no. Here they come again.

Slide. Wham. Crash. Bang. Another tangle of hands, feet, legs, and bodies.

At this rate, I thought, *not only am I going to upchuck all over everyone, but Mozart is going to be squashed to death. The rest of us will be black and blue—or whatever color k'roll k'pollies and fish-wishers get when they're bruised and battered.*

"Hey, you clumsy idiot," I yelled while I tried to wiggle out from under the pileup. "Don't damage the merchandise."

Groklan stopped suddenly. Ugor leaned back and sucked in his pudgy stomach to keep from bumping into him.

Tashee clamped her hands over my mouth. “Are you trying to get us killed?”

Turning around, Groklan bent forward. His red eyes glowed as he looked at us all heaped together in a corner of the cage.

I shrank back. Sometimes I can be really stupid. The others pressed against me.

“Give them to me,” Groklan said gruffly, taking the cage. With his other hand he punched Ugor in the head several times.

“Don’t damage the merchandise,” he roared.

“Yes, Master.”

“Take them and be more careful.” Groklan gave the cage back. “I need the fish-wisher in good condition for a while. At least until I’m ready to feed her to the g’slith g’slythe. I may find a use for the others too.”

“Yes, Master.”

When Groklan began walking again, Ugor stayed a step behind, cradling the cage in his arms.

“Master, may I ask a question?”

Groklan grunted and nodded his head.

“What about the k’roll k’pollies? May I have them when you’re done? Please, Master.”

The expression on Ugor’s face reminded me of a time I had dinner at Jimmy Grayson’s house. His dog sat by the table, begging for scraps. His eyes had this big, hopeful, pleading look, and his tongue lolled out the side of his mouth.

“You don’t take care of your pets,” Groklan said like a scolding parent. “When your last k’roll k’pollies got sick, they spread their illness to a dozen slaves. I don’t like throwing workers into the pit. It’s wasteful.”

“But this time—”

“No,” Groklan said firmly, “but if you’re very good, I’ll let you feed them to the nip-nappers.”

“Oh, thank you, Master. Thank you.”

Horror washed over me. I didn’t know what nip-nappers were, but being fed to anything didn’t sound very appealing.

“Did you hear that, Niklus?” Jonthun asked with his voice quivering. “He’s going to feed us to the nip-nappers.”

The brown on Niklus’s face faded to pale tan. He pressed his hands over his ears. "I heard. I heard."

"What are nip-nappers?" I asked Tashee.

"They're terrible little creatures," she told me. "They live in the ground and sleep most of the time. When they wake up, they're hungry. Then you'd better watch out. They'll swarm over you and nip, nip, nip until you're all gone."

"Oooooh," wailed Jonthun. "I don't want to get eaten."

"Maybe he'll change his mind," Niklus said. "Maybe he'll just push us into the pit."

"That would be better," I said encouragingly. "I could get us out of a hole, no matter how deep."

"Not possible," said Tashee. "No one gets out of the pit. It's magical. The bigger you are, the slower you fall. You starve to death before you hit the bottom."

"You're joking!"

My friends shook their heads.

Tears spilled down Jonthun's cheeks. "I don't want to starve to death."

"You like this better?" Using his thumbs and forefingers, Niklus pretended to pinch Jonthun's arms and legs. "Nip. Nip. Nip. Nip."

"Stop it!" Jonthun said, rolling away.

Devilment crept across Niklus's face, and he zoomed after him. "Nip. Nip. Nip."

"Cut it out, Niklus," I said.

"Nip-nappers don't cut, they nip," said Niklus. He reached for Jonthun again, and off they rolled, around and around.

Collapsing against the mesh of the cage, I shuddered. What a planet! Then I thought about some of the ways Sam has tormented me, and I realized things aren't so different here. A big brother is a big brother all through the universe.

On the k'roll k'pollies next circuit, I stuck my foot out in front of Niklus, and he bumped over it and screeched to a halt.

"Hey," he barked at me, "that hurt."

"Sorry," I said, "but we don't have time for this. Stop teasing Jonthun and start thinking. We've got to figure out how to get away from Groklan before anything bad happens to us."

"That's easy." Niklus shrugged. "You just need to learn how to use your magic."

Chapter 15
Curious Magic

I wished I had magic.

If I had, I'd make Groklan disappear and then I'd go home. I knew the wish-fish had tried and it had backfired, so maybe it was good I didn't have any magic I could mess up.

"Well," I said, "just in case I can't use my magic for anything helpful, let's come up with a Plan B."

"Plan B?" Tashee repeated in a puzzled voice.

"It's just a figure of speech," I explained. "It means let's come up with a second plan in case the first plan doesn't work."

"Oh." Tashee tapped her finger on her forehead. Then she tapped it on her teeth. After that, she tapped on her chin. It didn't look like it was helping.

Both k'roll k'pollies had their eyes closed and their faces scrunched up, as if thinking hurt. Who knows? Maybe it did.

When Groklan and Ugor reached the top of the staircase, they went down a long hall and stopped in front of a wide, double door. Guards in scarlet uniforms stood on each side of it.

They looked like ugly Christmas tree ornaments with their green skin and red clothes.

A guard pushed the doors open.

While Groklan climbed three steps to his black throne, Ugor set the cage on a table in the corner. He fumbled around in a cupboard until he produced two smaller cages.

Flipping the door open on our prison, he reached in and groped around. Niklus bounced from side to side, but Ugor caught him and put him in one of the other cages. Jonthun followed. Next Ugor nabbed me and shoved me into one by myself, leaving Tashee all alone in the big cage.

How could we escape if we were separated?

"I'll hear the first petitioner now, Ugor," Groklan said.

Leaving our individual jails close together on the tabletop, Ugor bowed and rushed from the room. After a moment, he brought in three grumpy g'nome g'nasties. One was hunched over and ancient looking. The other two were youngsters.

"State your business," Groklan said irritably.

"These two thieves stole d'apples from my tree," said the old one.

"It's our tree," said the other two together.

"It's mine. I planted it."

"On our land."

As the g'nome g'nasties argued, I looked over at Niklus and Jonthun. They clung to each other, shivering. Tashee had her hands over her face as if she was crying.

I wish I could do something for them, I thought. *They wouldn't be here if not for me.*

Pulling out my harmonica, I played the sad, lonely tune I'd composed in the park. The table we were on was far from the throne, and I thought maybe the boys and Tashee would find the music comforting. They'd been excited about it before.

Mozart jumped out of my pocket, ran up my arm, nuzzled my neck, and purred.

Tashee dropped her hands and smiled.

Niklus and Jonthun smiled too.

The room went silent except for the sound of my harmonica.

Then looking stunned, Tashee raised her arm with one finger aimed in Groklan's direction. Still playing, I turned so I could see what she was pointing at.

Groklan leaned forward in his chair.

Ugor had one foot raised as if he had started to climb the stairs to Groklan's throne.

The three grouchy g'nome g'nasties had their fists up, ready to punch each other, and two guards were reaching for them.

For several seconds, I just blew random notes on my harmonica, completely forgetting the tune I'd been playing.

I waited to see what would happen next.

Nothing did.

Every g'nome g'nasty was frozen in place.

Chapter 16

Who, What, Why, How?

"You discovered how to use your magic," whispered Tashee.

My mouth fell open and I forgot to blow.

The giants began moving and speaking again as if nothing had happened.

All except Groklan. He shook his head and gazed around, looking puzzled.

"I planted that tree over ten years ago," the old g'nome g'nasty shouted. He swung his arm and smacked one of the youngsters on the nose. A guard grabbed him and pulled him back.

"It's not our fault you were dumb enough to plant it on land you didn't own," the other young one shouted back.

"Timmy," Tashee said softly, "do it again."

Nodding, I played a few bars of the *Battle Hymn of the Republic.* As soon as I began, all the g'nome g'nasties became as stiff as green popsicles.

Tashee wiggled her finger at the k'roll k'pollies, and they bounced to the side of their cage closest to hers. "While Timmy freezes the g'nome g'nasties, I'll undo the locks. Then we can sneak away."

"Great." Niklus bounced up and down with joy. "We won't get thrown into the pit."

“Or nipped to death,” cried Jonthun, rolling around in circles.

Tashee began fiddling with her lock.

Lowering the harmonica, I whispered to her, “Not yet.”

“What?” squealed Niklus and Jonthun.

Released from the music’s spell, Groklan got a concerned expression on his face and peered in all directions. Because he was an evil magician, I thought, he might be able to sense the magic, even if he didn’t understand what it was or where it came from.

“Shhhh.” I glared at the k’roll k’pollies. “Right now there are too many g’nome g’nasties around.”

“But they’ll all be paralyzed when you start playing again,” Tashee said.

“Only the ones in here,” I said. “I could hear others moving around out in the hall.”

“Me, too,” Niklus admitted. “But as soon as we get there, they’ll turn into statues too, won’t they?”

“Yeah, but the ones in here will be free. If they notice we’re gone, they’ll look for us. Groklan might even be able to find us with his magic. We need to wait until he goes to bed. Even if he leaves a few guards, we’ll be able to get away then.”

Tashee giggled. “I’ll bet the guards will look a long time before waking up Groklan to tell him we’re gone.”

“Yeah,” Jonthun said with a wicked grin. “A real long time.”

“One more thing,” I said. “I can’t play the harmonica for hours and hours without resting. We need to see if it’ll work for you guys too.”

“We can’t do your magic,” Niklus said, shaking his head and putting his hands behind his back. “It wouldn’t be right.”

“Don’t be stupid,” I said. “When we were chased by the quird-birds, you shared your magic with Jonthun. You made him roll faster. This is the same thing.”

Stretching my arm between the bars, I offered Niklus the harmonica. “Try.”

When Niklus hesitated, Jonthun snatched it. “I’ll do it.” He slid his mouth up and down, blowing from high notes to low, then back again. The g’nome g’nasties moved in slow motion for a few seconds before they finally stopped.

“Let me try,” Tashee said.

Huff puff. Again. Huff puff. Blow. Bluster. Gasp.

Not a sound except Tashee's breathing.

"You've got to close your lips around it," I told her. "All the air is getting away."

"You're joking." Tashee shook her finger at me, scolding. "You want me to put it in my mouth? After the k'roll k'pollie slobbered all over it?"

"I did not," Jonthun said, folding his arms over his big belly and frowning at her.

"Just wipe it off," I said.

"I'll do it." Jonthun grabbed the harmonica and rubbed it on his shirt.

"My turn," said Niklus.

Jonthun shook his head.

"You and Tashee already got to try," said Niklus. "It's my turn."

"Nope." Jonthun began playing again. Just notes. Not a tune. But it was enough. The g'nome g'nasties didn't move.

"Give it to me!" Niklus grabbed the harmonica. Jonthun held on tight. Niklus tried to shake him off by bouncing to the top of the cage. Jonthun wouldn't let go.

Mozart became agitated as the brothers argued. He hopped around on my shoulder, making a sound like a high pitched snarl.

Niklus spun around. Jonthun hit one side of the cage, bounced off, and hit the other. He still held on. Niklus rolled over, pulling Jonthun along.

"Give it to me," Niklus said angrily.

"No. You said you didn't want to."

"Now I do."

"Too late." Jonthun said in a smug tone.

Groklan slammed his fists down on the arms of his throne. "Enough!" he roared.

With a yap, Mozart dove back into my pocket.

Niklus and Jonthun skidded to a stop.

Jonthun snatched the harmonica from Niklus and held it behind his back. Then he sidled over to the bars and passed it to Tashee, smirking all the while.

The king giant rose with his fists on his hips. His brows were pinched together, and his red eyes glowed very bright. He stared at the three arguing g'nome g'nasties. "Since you can't agree on who owns the d'apple tree, I claim it for myself."

"But—but—," sputtered the old man.

Groklan continued talking without paying any attention. "All three of you will help gather the fruit and bring it to the palace. Then you can buy back anything you want. That's fair."

"Actually, your Majesty—" a young g'nome g'nasty said.

Groklan gave the speaker an annoyed scowl. "If you disagree with me, I'll give you two choices: the pit or the nip-nappers."

The three men bowed with their knees knocking together.

"Quite fair, your Majesty," the two youngsters said, their voices squeaky and scared.

"Yes, indeed," said the old man, wiping his forehead with a handkerchief in a trembling hand. "Couldn't be fairer."

"I like my subjects to be happy," Groklan said. He pulled his lips back in an ugly grin. "You are dismissed."

The three scurried out.

Groklan said, "I won't hear any more complaints today. Have the guards send the others away."

While Ugor rushed to the door and passed on the orders, Groklan crossed to the table. He picked up my cage, held it high, and gave it a shake.

I tumbled head over heels.

"The wish-fish said a strange creature would defeat me if I couldn't figure out its power. Is this it?" Groklan asked.

"Yes, Master," Ugor said, coming up behind him. "Remember the image in the magic mirror. It looked just like this thing."

"I don't sense any magic." Groklan handed the cage to Ugor. "Take it out and give it to me."

I tried to dodge this way and that, but Ugor's big green fingers caught me.

Groklan held me up to the light. He held me to his ear. He sniffed me.

Then he opened up his mouth.

Holy cow, I thought, *he's going to take a bite out of me.*

Squirming as hard as I could, I expected to lose a hand or a foot at least. Instead, Groklan stuck out his long green tongue and licked my face.

Oh barf! He needs to brush his teeth and gargle with mouthwash.

He licked me again, all the way from my feet to my hair.

"Mmmmmmmmm." He smacked his lips as if he'd tasted something delicious.

He's going to eat me!

Chapter 17

Harmonica Hopscotch

But he didn't.

He rolled his tongue around in his mouth the way I do when Mom lets me have a chocolate from the big box Dad always gives her on Valentine's Day. They're always creams and jellies, and sometimes you can't tell the strawberry from the raspberry without real concentration.

That's what Groklan was doing. He was trying to identify my flavor.

"Did you find the magic, Master?" Ugor asked eagerly.

"No. He has a magic ring, but its powers are puny. It lets him fly. Ha. Ha. Horses can fly. That won't help him defeat me."

Groklan dropped me into Ugor's hand.

"Put him back."

"Can I feed the k'roll k'pollies to the nip-nappers now?" Ugor asked while he put me back in the pen.

"No. Maybe its powers work through its friends. Get me the fish-wisher."

Oh no! She has the harmonica.

I stumbled toward her.

"What'll we do? What'll we do?" Niklus and Jonthun bounced

back and forth, from side to side. I wanted to scream at them that this was no time to panic.

“I think the k’roll k’pollies are getting nervous, Ugor,” Groklan said with a chuckle.

“Yes, Master.” Ugor reached for Tashee.

Cowering in a corner, she had her hands behind her back. “No, no, no,” she cried dramatically.

“Tashee!” Niklus slammed against the bars and stretched out his arms. Something flew through the air from Tashee’s cage. Niklus closed his fingers around it.

As Groklan sniffed Tashee, Niklus opened his hand and winked at me.

He had the harmonica.

I grinned and gave him a thumbs-up.

“Just a regular fish-wisher,” Groklan said. “A little magic like all fish-wishers. Nothing special. Get me the big k’roll k’pollie.”

Niklus’s eyes bulged as he looked at the harmonica he held. As if his brain had stopped working, he began bouncing all over the place.

“Give it to me. Give it to me,” Jonthun whispered loudly. As Niklus’s terror worsened, Jonthun matched him, bounce for bounce. His hand was extended as he tried to grab the harmonica.

When Ugor put Tashee back, he swept her cage to the side. Then he picked up the one the k’roll k’pollies was in. He swished his hand around inside.

Niklus bounced faster and faster.

Jonthun tackled him.

Ooooomph! Niklus slammed the cage bottom, and the air swooshed out of his lungs. He dropped the harmonica.

Jonthun ran and jumped on it, but he slipped and ricocheted.

Whappity. Whappity. Whap. He hit the other side, the roof, the floor, the side again.

“I’ve never bothered to watch k’roll k’pollies play before,” Groklan said, taking the cage from Ugor and holding it at eye level. “They’re very entertaining. I understand now why they’re your favorite pets.”

Lowering the cage, he held it while Ugor grabbed Niklus. As soon as the door clacked shut, Jonthun rolled over to the bars and held up the harmonica.

I sighed with relief. Then Groklan set the cage down, and I

groaned in hopelessness.

Before, all the cages had been close together. Now, he set the k'roll k'pollie cage at the edge of the table, a good six or seven feet away from its previous position.

One sniff and Groklan handed Niklus back to Ugor. "This one has even less magic than the fish-wisher. Get me the little one."

When Ugor opened the door, it stuck, and he gave it a quick jerk.

Jonthun slipped and banged into the bars.

The harmonica slipped from his fingers.

Turning end over end, it somersaulted out of the cage.

Chapter 18

The Great Escape

Boom!

The harmonica hit the table with a clap as loud as thunder.

My heart did flip-flops as I waited for Ugor to pick it up and give it to Groklan. As soon as the big giant touched it, he'd know it was magic.

We'd never escape.

"There you go," Ugor said. He rolled Niklus across the bottom of the cage like a marble, and then grabbed Jonthun.

Neither g'nome g'nasty paid any attention to the harmonica. I swallowed my heart back into place and let myself breathe. To the giants, the harmonica probably hadn't made any more noise than a pin dropping.

Groklan held Jonthun to his nose. Sniff. Sniff.

"He has no more magic than the others. Put him back."

Groklan crossed to some shelves and began pulling down books and making a stack of them on another table. "Somewhere there must be a spell I can use to figure out how the creature's magic works."

"May I have the k'roll—?"

"No!" Groklan snapped with irritation. "If I can't find a spell tonight, I may have to do some tests on them. Get my supper and take it to my room. I'll be up in a few minutes. Then go to bed." Groklan flipped a few pages. As Ugor left, he called out, "Post a couple guards of in here."

"Yes, Master."

Now that Groklan was focused on other things, I turned my attention to my harmonica. Could I reach it? It was halfway between my cage and the k'roll k'pollies. Three and a half feet, maybe four feet.

"You big lump!" Niklus said. He gave Jonthun a swat. "You just had to drop Timmy's magic, didn't you?"

"I'm not a lump," Jonthun wailed, rolling away. "I didn't do it on purpose."

Slam!

Groklan banged the book closed. He opened a different one.

Scowling at Groklan then at Jonthun, Niklus whispered, "You dropped it, you figure out how to get it." He put his fists on the sides of his fat stomach. "Go on. Get it."

"All right." Jonthun rolled to the bars and reached. Not even close. He took a deep breath, blew out all the air, and flattened his stomach as much as he could.

He lay on the floor and stuck his arm out again. A little closer. He stretched and stretched and stretched. He rolled to a sitting position. "I can't reach it. My arms aren't long enough."

"You big lump. I'll just have to get it myself."

Niklus backed up as far as he could.

Run. Jump. He grabbed between the bars.

Bounce. Whack. He hit the other side of the cage.

Groklan glanced up, and for a moment everyone stood perfectly still, not wanting to draw his attention.

When he went back to his book, Tashee said quietly, "Niklus, you don't have to—"

"Shhh. I'm busy." He rolled over to the bars. He lay on his stomach, blew the air out as Jonthun had earlier, and reached. He wiggled his fingers, trying to make them longer.

"Maybe I should push." Jonthun put his shoulder to Niklus's rump and shoved. Again. Again.

Niklus's body bulged between the bars like a marshmallow smashed by a fork. His face went dark, darker, darkest.

"Stop!" I waved my arms and jumped around, but Jonthun ignored me. I yelled as loud as I dared with Groklan there. "I don't think he can breathe, Jonthun."

"Sure, he can." Jonthun pushed again.

"He's going black."

"Uh oh!" Jonthun rolled into a corner.

Pop!

Niklus flew backward. Grooves from the bars were etched into his body.

Pop! Pop! Pop! The grooves disappeared. Niklus's belly was as round as a beach ball again.

"Grrrrrr!" He launched himself at Jonthun.

In a flash, Jonthun rolled up the side of the cage, across the top, and down the other side. Niklus spun around.

"I was just trying to help," Jonthun said. He plopped down on his bottom. "I dropped Timmy's magic because I was trying to help. I almost squished you to death because I was trying to help." He began crying. "I can't do anything right. Now we'll all get thrown into the pit or fed to the nip-nappers."

"Aw, don't cry." Niklus bounced over and patted Jonthun's arm. "It's not your fault. It could've happened to anyone."

Wiping his face with his hand, Jonthun sniffled. "I'm sorry."

"I know," Niklus said. "We'll think of something else. Don't worry."

"Timmy," Tashee called in a loud whisper. "As soon as Groklan leaves, I'll—"

"Just a minute, Tashee," I said. I turned to Jonthun. "Niklus is right. It's not your fault. Maybe I can get it. I don't have a big belly to get in the way."

"Please try," Jonthun said. "If you can reach it, everything will be all right."

"But Timmy," Tashee whispered, "if you'll just be patient for a minute, I can—"

"You can't reach it," I said, frowning at Tashee because I was getting tired of all her interruptions. "You're even farther away than I am."

Lying down, I stuck my arm between the bars and reached as hard as I could. I felt like I might dislocate my shoulder, but I could tell I wasn't even close. "Tashee, you said part of your magic is moving things. That's how you open locks. Can you move my cage forward a little?"

"No." Tashee's arms were folded and her foot went tap, tap, tap on the floor. "It's too big." She sounded bored.

"All right, I'll just have to do it myself." I grabbed the bars and shook them, thinking I might make the cage jump forward a bit.

Scrape. Scratch. Scruff.

The cage moved.

I jumped back.

"Which one of you did that?" I asked, glaring.

"Not me," Tashee said, covering a yawn with her hand.

"Niklus? Jonthun?"

"No way."

Groklan put down the book he was reading.

I grabbed the bars to keep from collapsing with fear. He must have heard the cage move.

No. He was leaving. He snatched up the pile of books, opened the door, and was gone.

I had an exciting thought.

If Tashee, Niklus or Jonthun didn't move the cage, I must have. How'd I do it? I don't have any magic except the harmonica and the—

Yes! The ring.

Pressing it against a bar, I told it, *Ring, forward.*

Gradually the cage moved. An inch. Two inches.

"It'll take me a while," I said, "but I can shift the cage with the ring."

"Would you mind a little help?" Tashee offered.

"You're too far away!" Niklus, Jonthun and I all exclaimed at the same time.

"True, but—" Sticking her fingers in the lock, Tashee wiggled around.

Click.

She pushed open the door, got the harmonica, and handed it to me. "I tried to tell you," she said.

I could have died.

Of all the stupid things I've ever said or done, this might have been the worst. "Uh, thanks" was all I could think to tell her.

Footsteps in the hall saved me from having to say more.

“Uh oh,” Tashee said, “someone’s coming.”

“We have to spend the night in here,” a sleepy voice said as two guards entered.

Tashee dashed back to her cage.

The guards shut the big, double doors behind them.

“At least we have privacy if we decide to snooze a little.”

While one guard arranged chairs along the opposite side of the room from us, the other went around snuffing out candles until only a couple were left burning.

I motioned with my hand, and Tashee and the k’roll k’pollies stepped closer.

“As soon as they get settled,” I whispered, “I’ll start playing the harmonica. Tashee, you unlock the cages. Niklus, as soon as you and Jonthun are free, bounce down to the floor and see if you can find rags, scraps of paper, twigs, or anything that we can arrange in our cages to make them think we’re still here. It’s pretty dark with the candles out. Maybe they won’t realize we’re gone until morning.”

“What a great idea,” Tashee said.

“I saw it in *Escape from Alcatraz,*” I said, smiling. Maybe I wasn’t so dumb after all.

“You saw it where?”

“In a movie.”

“Movie?”

“Never mind.” The guards were lounging in their chairs, and I started playing.

As soon as Tashee undid the locks, Niklus and Jonthun bounced around the room, gathering dust bunnies, bits of trash, and other odds and ends. When they had an armful, they helped Tashee position the clumps so they looked like bodies.

“Let’s go,” Tashee said. She climbed onto my back, and while I continued playing, I used the magic ring to float us to the ground. What came next?

Those huge, double doors were closed. And they opened inward. I couldn’t use the ring to push them open.

Bouncing higher and higher, Niklus checked the windows. Jonthun rolled around the walls and across the ceiling looking for a crack big enough that we could squeeze through.

I wandered around blowing on the harmonica, wondering if we

had escaped from a small prison just to get trapped in a large one. We had to get out of here.

"Let's hide under that chair," Tashee suggested, "so we can talk. We need to decide what to do."

A creaking sound came from the wall.

A panel flipped open.

"Get in here," a high, muffled voice demanded.

Chapter 19

Into the Walls

The opening in the wall was a black square.

"Hurry," the voice said. Pale hands came out of the dark and grabbed Niklus. "We need to hurry."

"Hey! Let go." Niklus jerked backward with such force he pulled the owner of the hands off balance.

Bump. Jostle. Bounce.

A k'roll k'pollie thumped into the room, knocking Niklus into Jonthun, Jonthun into Tashee, and Tashee into me. A basket tumbled onto the floor.

Surprised, I almost dropped the harmonica. But I quickly got over my shock and began playing again.

The new k'roll k'pollie sat on the floor and looked around. "Why aren't the guards moving? What's that sound?"

"I'll ask the questions," Tashee said, pushing her way to the front. "Who are you and what are you doing here?"

"My name is Jesska." She rolled to her feet and brushed herself off. Anyway I guessed she was a girl. I wasn't going to ask. She was peach colored, shorter than Niklus but taller than Jonthun. On her head, instead of hair or quills or fuzz, were curls that looked like they'd been cut from a bright orange plastic slinky.

Jesska goggled at Tashee. "You're a fish-wisher."

"Of course I am. Are you a spy? Whose side are you on? What are you doing here?"

"Don't get snooty," Jesska said with her nose in the air. *She's a girl all right. Just like Brittney.* "I'm a slave, and right now I'm trying to save your lives."

With a sickening puppy-love expression, Niklus said, "You can save my life."

"And mine," Jonthun said, hopping in front of his brother and shoving him aside. "You're beautiful."

Smiling, Jesska patted Jonthun's cheek.

Niklus turned away and kicked the basket Jesska had dropped. His jealousy quickly turned to happiness. "Swamp fruit! Great. I'm starved."

Jesska snatched the basket and the fruit away from him. "It's not for you. I was on my way to feed Pink-Dotted Bertie when I heard you bouncing around in here."

"There's a wish-fish in Groklan's palace?" cried Tashee.

Jesska nodded. "It's my job to gather fruit to feed her. I'm already late." She stepped back through the opening in the wall. "Hurry before the guards wake up. We can talk in the tunnel."

Jonthun quickly followed, gazing at her in adoration. I almost expected him to float in the air with little pink hearts surrounding him, like in cartoons.

"Don't worry about the guards," Niklus said, trying to push past his brother. "The magic music puts them under a spell."

I glanced at Tashee.

I wished I could put down the danged harmonica and ask a few hundred questions.

Tashee shrugged. "We have to get out of here somehow. Besides, I want to know more about Pink-Dotted Bertie. Why isn't she in the swamp where she belongs?"

Still blowing a tune, I shrugged back at her.

Tashee nodded toward the tunnel, and together we stepped into the darkness.

As soon as Jesska shut the panel, I put the harmonica in my pocket and took a deep breath.

Jesska mumbled a few words and a soft glow appeared in the palm of her hand. She carried the basket with the other. "Follow me. There's a place up ahead where the tunnel is wider. We can sit and talk for a moment. I've got lots of questions."

"So do we," said Tashee.

As we walked, every now and then, I felt the top of my hair brush against the low ceiling. I didn't have to lift my hands very far to feel the walls on both sides. A shiver skipped up and down my back.

Craning my neck, I tried to see the light Jesska carried, but all I saw was a dim outline of Niklus.

I don't like the dark. I absolutely, completely, totally hate small spaces. And here I was in a tiny, almost pitch black place. Goosebumps popped up on my arms.

"Where are we?" I asked, thinking I might not feel so creeped out if there was some conversation.

"We're inside the castle walls," Jesska said. "These tunnels were made centuries ago by little people who served as messengers for the old kings. We don't know what happened to them. They all just disappeared."

"So," I said, "the palace was empty for a long time before the g'nome g'nasties moved in?"

"Right."

"I don't like it in here," Niklus grumbled. "I can barely —oomph!"

I bumped into him. Tashee bumped into me.

Niklus grunted and groaned. "Uuumph. Grrrr. Mmumph."

"What's the matter?" I asked. "Are you hurt?"

No comment.

"Hey, you guys," Jonthun called. "Hurry up. There's a big spot up here, kind of like a room."

Niklus didn't move.

"What's wrong," I asked again.

"I'm stuck."

"Stuck!" Tashee's voice came from behind me. "Just like a k'roll k'pollie. You can't take them anywhere. Timmy, give him a shove."

"I don't know if I should. I don't want to hurt him."

"It's all right," Niklus said. "Maybe it'll help."

I put my shoulder to Niklus's back and pushed.

"Let me help," said Tashee.

Shove. Press. Heave. Jostle.

He didn't budge.

"Now what?" I asked.

"Try again," Jonthun said. "I'll pull."

Yank. Ram. Struggle. Strain.

"He is such a—such a k'roll k'pollie," said Tashee, panting for breath. "It's like trying to move a wall."

Niklus gave a long sigh. "I'll just stay here until I die. Climb over me. Leave me all alone in the dark to starve."

"We're not going to leave you," I said. "Let me think." I slumped against the wall. When I was pushing Niklus, it was a familiar sensation, like I'd done something similar before. What was it?

"I've got it. He's not like a wall. He's like a water balloon. We push on his back, and his sides spread out, wedging him in tighter."

"Well, that's it then," Tashee said. "We'll just have to climb over him, like he said. The ceiling's a little higher here. We should be able to squeeze by."

"No," I told her. "We need to push his sides in, so the bulgy parts are in the front and back. That ought to loosen him up. If we stand back to back, Tashee, you can work your arms between him and the wall on that side, and I'll do the same on this side. You push toward me, and I push toward you."

"Eeeeeiiiiouuuuu, gross!" Tashee squealed.

"Come on. Help me."

For a minute, I thought she was going to refuse.

Finally she mumbled unhappily, "Oh, all right." She reached out and smacked Niklus. "You'd better appreciate this!"

When we'd worked our arms between Niklus and the wall, I called to Jonthun, "Get ready to pull. Now, Tashee, push in with your arms and give his behind a shove with your hip. All together. One, two, three. Now!"

Swoosh!

Like a spitball shot from a rubber band, Niklus blasted out.

Slam.

He flew into Jonthun.

Bam.

Jonthun smacked into Jesska.

Bounce. Bounce. Bouncity. Bounce.

From the glow in Jesska's hand, I watched the three of them bump and bash their way down the tunnel, disappear, then spring back into view.

"They must've reached the big room Jonthun told us about," Tashee said. She shook her head and murmured as she tromped on, "It was bad enough with two of them. Now we've got three. Someday one of them will squash us flat."

I stopped to pick up Jesska's basket, and Tashee put the fruit back into it.

We reached the large chamber, which looked as if it was made of cinderblocks, just as the k'roll k'pollies spun to a stop.

Long ago, a few chunks had tumbled from the walls, and Jesska leaned against one. The brothers sat back to back, supporting each other. They looked like they'd had a rough time of it, banging into walls, ground, and ceiling, out of control.

"Are you The Chosen One?" Jesska asked me.

"I don't think so," I said. I handed her back the basket then sat on a block and rested against the wall.

"Of course he is," Tashee said. "His magic music makes the g'nome g'nasties so they can't move or speak or hear or anything."

"That ought to help," Jesska said, "if it's used right." She bounced to her feet. "I wish we had more time to talk, but it'll have to wait. I think I heard something behind us. We'd better go."

"We're not going anywhere," Tashee said with her hands clenched into fists, "until you answer some questions. Like, what're you doing in a secret tunnel if you're a slave? And where did you get swamp fruit? And where is Pink-Dotted Bertie?"

"Later. We've got to get out of here. Come on."

"Not on your life," Tashee said, stamping her foot.

"Shhh," I told her. "I heard something back there too. Something dragging on the ground."

"We waited too long," Jesska wailed. She grabbed the basket of fruit and Tashee's hand. "Hurry. Hurry. Maybe we can outrun it if we hurry."

Scrape. Slither. Scratch.

"Sssomeone isss near. I hear voicesss."

"I ssseee a light. Who isss it?"

"Sssomeone sssmall. Sssomeone who fitsss in our ssspace."

There was a pause.

"Sssomeone sssnack sssize."

Chapter 20

Twisting and Twining

As Jesska ran down a side tunnel, she kept a firm hold on Tashee, who had a tight grip on me. Niklus and Jonthun rolled and bounced behind. Jesska had released her light so it floated overhead instead of resting in her hand.

"Ssstupid sssnake. You ssscared it off."

"Ssshhh. Lisssten. Footstepsss."

Excitement sounded in the answer. "Ssseveral."

"Not sssnacks. Sssupper!"

Dropping Tashee's hand, Jesska paused at a fork in the tunnel and took a few steps each way, peering into the darkness.

"Fassster."

"Don't let them essscape."

Slink. Scoot. Slide.

The sound of dragging scales quickened.

Finally, Jesska turned left. The tunnel sloped downward, and she began to roll headfirst with her arms stuck straight out to the sides. The basket twirled around in her hand, fast enough that not a single fruit dropped out.

Niklus and Jonthun rolled after her.

The best Tashee and I could do was run as quickly as our legs would carry us.

"Thisss way," the snake's voice sounded.

Another fork.

Jesska barely slowed down.

Off she whirled to the right.

The slope became steeper.

Whoosh. Run. Bounce. Roll. Zip. Zap.

On and on we fled.

My side hurt. My legs felt as if they'd buckle soon.

I wanted to use the magic ring to carry me, but although the tunnel had widened at the sides, the ceiling was still low and the path was full of twists and turns. If I smacked into one, I wouldn't bounce like a k'roll k'pollie. I'd kill myself.

Finally Jesska rolled to a stop. We clustered around her.

Gasp. Wheeze. Rasp. Crackle. Huff. Puff.

My heart thumped like the drums in a heavy-metal band. My breath howled like a punk-rock singer.

Even the k'roll k'pollies were panting. They looked like balloons being blown up, having half the air released, and being blown up again. And again.

After a few minutes, Jesska whispered, "Do you hear anything?"

I held my breath and listened. So did the others.

One by one we shook our heads.

"Me, neither." Jesska sat on the ground and looked at the basket she held. "Poor Pink-Dotted Bertie. And the other one. I didn't feed them. Now, they'll start getting weak again."

"Two!" Tashee said, gawking. "You've got two wish-fish?"

"I've only seen Pink-Dotted Bertie, but she told me she shares her food with another. He keeps hidden in some plants at the bottom of the bowl."

"What are they doing here?" Tashee demanded. "Why aren't they in the swamp?"

"Groklan caught them."

"Impossible."

"I know," Jesska said, sadly, "but it's true."

Tashee opened her mouth. She closed it again. Opened it. Closed it. Then she slumped against the wall and buried her face in her hands. "Oh, poor wish-fish. This is terrible. What'll we do?"

"One thing at a time," I said, putting my arm around Tashee's shoulders. "We'll find a way to help Pink-Dotted Bertie and the other wish-fish." I looked over at Jesska. "How do we get out of here without bumping into the g'slith g'slythe?"

Biting her lip, Jesska peered up and down the tunnel. It was completely black beyond her dim glow. "I'm not sure."

"Not sure?" I repeated. "You led us here."

"That was just to get away from the snake." She looked all around. "I've never come this far before. I don't know where we are."

"Oh, that's perfect," Tashee said sarcastically, dropping her hands from her face. "Of all the dumb tricks. Why didn't you tell us you didn't know where you were going? We'd have been better off without you."

Jesska's lower lip began to tremble and a tear sneaked down each peach-colored cheek. "I was trying to help."

"Well, you didn't."

Niklus bounced between the two girls. "Leave her alone," he told Tashee.

"You made her cry," Jonthun said as he rolled next to his brother. "Say you're sorry."

"What!" Tashee turned to me like I was the referee. "Did you hear that? She gets us lost, and they want *me* to apologize to *her*. Of all the nerve!"

Niklus turned to me too. "Tell her she has to."

Sniffling, Jesska said, "Maybe I ought to just leave."

"Why don't you?" Tashee snarled and glared at her.

"Don't you talk to her like that," Niklus yelled.

"You better be nice!" hollered Jonthun.

The three k'roll k'pollies and Tashee waved their arms, stomped their feet, shook their fingers, made faces, and snapped at each other.

Watching and listening to them made my stomach hurt.

We were in Groklan's castle.

We were lost.

The g'slith g'slythe was searching for us.

As soon as the guards noticed we were gone, they'd start searching for us too.

I wasn't at all sure we'd live long enough to help Prince Seth, which meant all the adult k'nick k'nockers and k'roll k'pollies would die. Maybe everyone on this whole planet except the g'nome g'nasties would die.

I'd die here too.

"Shut up," I shouted.

Four pairs of eyes blinked at me with surprise.

Tashee started to say something, but I said, "Shhh, not a word. Not a single word."

Tashee's mouth snapped shut.

"Argue later if you have to," I said, "but we're in serious danger." I had their attention now. "Just because we don't know where we are, that doesn't mean the g'slith g'slythe can't find us. We need to figure out what to do."

"What are you?" Jesska asked me as she wiped tears from her face. "I thought you were The Chosen One, but you're not as tall as a k'nick k'nocker or as round as a k'roll k'pollie. You're too nice and polite to be a fish-wisher. And you're obviously not a g'nome g'nasty or a wish-fish."

"He's not from Shalamar," Niklus answered before I could. "The k'nick k'nocker king made a ring that brought him here. He's a human from planet Earth."

"Right," Jesska said with her lips curled up in a tiny smile. "He climbed right out of a book of fairytales, huh?"

"Earth isn't a fairytale," I told her. "I'd love to tell you about it sometime, but first, we have to get out of these tunnels. Do you have any idea which way we should go?"

"The slaves are kept underground. If we keep going down, I think we'll find them eventually."

"All right," I said. "Lead on."

"Will you trust me," Jesska asked, staring straight at Tashee.

Frowning, Tashee scraped her foot across the floor.

"It doesn't matter," I said. "You know the castle and the tunnels and we don't. You have to be the leader."

Slither. Sneak. Skid. Skulk.

A hissing voice whispered, "I'm sssure the outburssst came from thisss direction."

"The echoesss confussse me, but I can tassste them with my tongue. They are clossse."

"Sssilence. Don't ssscare them again."

Chapter 21

Between a Rock and a Deep Place

I pressed my finger to my lips.

Motioning toward the darkness, I said right in Niklus's ear. "Roll, don't bounce." I repeated the same thing to the other k'roll k'pollies.

Putting my arms around Tashee, I lifted her while I thought up and forward. I didn't dare have her ride piggyback. I might misjudge a distance and accidentally scrape her off.

Ahead, the path's slope became steeper. The k'roll k'pollies zoomed down it like rubber balls on a slippery slide. If it had been a bit smoother, I might have tried sliding down it myself.

"Which passsage?" the snake hissed somewhere behind us.

"Thisss one."

Somehow Jesska managed to split her light, so part of it floated in front of me. I appreciated it because the tunnel bent left then right. After a brief straight stretch, it twisted right then left. I used all my concentration not to bash into walls.

At one point, Mozart peered out of my pocket. Immediately he dove for cover again.

"I can't sssee them. I can't sssmell them. Are you sssure thisss isss the right way?"

"I'm sssure. We'll find sssupper sssoon."

The snake's voices grew fainter.

"I'll ssstarve if we don't find them fassst."

My arms were beginning to hurt. Tashee wasn't really very heavy, but the longer I held her, the heavier she seemed to become. I had to rest.

"Jesska, wait a minute."

The k'roll k'pollies spun to a stop.

"What's the matter," Niklus asked quietly.

Jonthun looked at me suspiciously. "You're not tired already, are you?"

"Just my arms," I said without thinking.

Tashee took offense. "Are you saying I'm fat?"

"Of course not."

"You want me to stop eating so I'll be skinny like those creatures in Earthling fairytales. What do you call them? Supper-something? No, it's…it's…supermodels. You want me too look like a supermodel?"

"No, no," I protested. "You're perfect just the way you are."

"I am?" Tashee said, glowing with delight. "Do you really think so?"

My face burned. I'm sure I cycled through a dozen shades of red. I needed something to do other than watching Tashee beam at me. So I reached into my pocket and rubbed Mozart on the head. When I removed my hand, he climbed halfway out of my pocket. He looked like he wanted to jump up onto my shoulder. He opened his mouth for a loud yip.

Leaning forward, Tashee whispered to him. He disappeared into my pocket again.

"What did you say to him," I asked.

"I told him we were hiding from the g'slith g'slythe. It doesn't usually eat fuzzle-wuzzles—they're too small—except when it's really hungry. Then it'll eat anything." She batted her eyelashes at me. "Now, back to what we were discussing. What do you think is my best feature?"

I was saved from having to answer by a tug on my sleeve.

Niklus pointed at a wedge shaped crack in the wall. "There's light coming out of there."

I peered closely. "I think you're right. I'll go see."

"I'll come too," said Tashee.

"Me too," Niklus and Jonthun said together.

"Better let me check it out first," I said. "It might be dangerous."

"Also someone might get stuck," Tashee said.

Jonthun swatted Niklus on the arm. "You big lump," he said.

It didn't take me long. Within minutes, I was back.

"The crack leads to a short tunnel that opens up on a long corridor. The hallway has torches in holders along the walls. I guess that means guards or servants use this area. We'll need to keep our eyes and ears open. If you take a look, Jesska, maybe you'll recognize where we are."

Nodding, she slipped into the crack, leaving a bit of glow light behind for us. Tashee followed but came right back.

"Well," Niklus said. "Can I get through?"

"It's kind of small," Tashee said. "Jonthun will probably just fit."

"What about me?" Niklus grabbed Jonthun's hand. He looked over his shoulder into the darkness. "You wouldn't just leave me for the g'slith g'slythe, would you?"

"What do you think, Tashee," I asked.

"Well, if we leave him, he'll get eaten and we won't. That sounds fair to me."

Horrified, Niklus started bouncing in agitation.

I glared at Tashee. "I meant do you think we can help him squeeze through like we did before?"

Niklus bounced faster. "Don't leave me."

"We won't," I said firmly. "Jonthun, you can go on through. Tashee and I will take up the rear. Uh, I mean, we'll go last in case we have to push."

Squeeze. Stuff. Shove. Squish. Squash.

Niklus popped through the crack. He hit the wall, shot into the corridor, and slammed into Jonthun and Jesska.

When Tashee and I entered the hallway, we found ourselves surrounded by rebounding k'roll k'pollies.

Jonthun rolled between us, shoving me to one side and Tashee to the other.

Tashee skipped around trying to keep upright, but Jesska ricocheted off the wall, knocked her over, and went bouncing away. Before Tashee could clamber to her feet, Niklus, who was spiraling out of control, bumped into her and flattened her again.

Covering her head with her arms, Tashee lay on the ground. When the bouncing stopped, she stood, brushed dirt off her scales, and glared at me like it was all my fault.

"I want to go back to the swamp," she said, "before I get finally and permanently killed by runaway k'roll k'pollies."

"Hey," Jesska called. "There are some stairs over here. Maybe they lead to the slave pens." She blew on her hand, and both the glows that she'd made went out. Then she started down.

We followed.

Our luck is getting better, I thought. *We have light, we're out of the tunnels, and we're going in the right direction.*

At the bottom of the steps was a big door, partway open.

Inside, it was as dark as the tunnels in the walls.

I told the ring to take me up so I could grab a torch.

"Why don't you make that glow again?" Tashee asked Jesska.

After she did, the four of them stepped through the door together. I wasn't far behind them.

"It's a big room," Niklus said.

As I entered, light spread out from the torch, much brighter than Jesska's glow.

I looked around.

The room was long and narrow. In the middle of the floor, crowding the walls on two sides, was a round dark spot that my torchlight couldn't reach.

Standing in front of it, stiff with fright, were Tashee and the three k'roll k'pollies.

"What is it?" I asked.

They answered in chorus, "The pit."

Chapter 22

Ssstare or Ssstarve

Cautiously, Tashee and the k'roll k'pollies backed away from the huge hole in the floor.

"Let's get out of here," I cried, turning and running for the door.

It was blocked by a long blue shape with green and yellow splotches. Red eyes stared into mine.

I froze.

"Sssupper isss ready," the g'slith g'slythe hissed.

"We mussst make sssure none of it getsss away."

Chuckling, the snake twisted its double tail together.

WHACK!

It slammed the door shut.

From where I stood, I could see the door had no doorknob or latch on this side.

"Dibsss on the fish-wisssher," one head yelled.

"That isss sssatisfactory," the other head told it. "I want thisss ssstranger, anyway. It isss clossser, ssso I'll get to eat firssst."

"Run, Timmy," Tashee yelled.

I tried to, but I couldn't pry my eyes away from the snake.

I was bound as completely as if they'd tied me up with rope.

Red eyes floated closer.

Soon the blue body would start coiling around me.

Oooomph!

Something smacked me in the back and knocked me over. I dropped the torch as I rolled sideways.

"Don't look in its eyes," Niklus said. He grabbed my hand and pulled me up.

"This way." Tashee waved her hand toward the far side of the long room. In the shadows, I could just make out another door, a green one with a brass handle.

Although the pit almost reached the side walls, there was just enough floor space for a small person to scoot by on. With her back pressed to the wall, Tashee was already side-stepping past.

"The torch," I cried out. Lying on the floor, the flame had begun to sputter. I definitely didn't want to be in a dark room with a pit and a g'slith g'slythe.

In an instant, Jonthun rolled forward.

"Got it." He bounced up and lit several torches that were in brackets on the wall. Then he rolled across the ceiling and came down beside the green door.

"Go on," Niklus called to me. "I'll keep it busy."

"We'll both keep it busy," Jesska said with a shy grin.

As I inched across the narrow ledge, Niklus and Jessica dribbled around, over, and on top of the g'slith g'slythe.

It jerked its heads around, trying to paralyze the k'roll k'pollies with its hypnotic eyes, but Niklus and Jesska were careful to avoid its gaze.

"Ssstop where you are."

"Hold ssstill."

Bounce. Bounce.

Niklus hopped over the snake's back, punched one head so it smacked into the other, and then bounced away.

Bounce. Bounce.

Jesska landed on the tails.

Snarl. Snip. Snap. One head opened its mouth and tried to catch Jesska.

Jump. Spring. Leap. Jesska got away.

"Ssstupid sssnake, you missed."

"Don't criticizzze me, you lazzzy thing. At leassst, I tried."

Niklus and Jesska huddled together and whispered.

Then, around and around and around the g'slith g'slythe they rolled. Faster and faster.

The snake's heads whipped back and forth, back and forth.

All at once, Niklus and Jesska bounced up and landed together on the g'slith g'slythe's back.

Whoosh! All the snake's air escaped.

Running forward, holding hands, Niklus and Jesska jumped and bounced at the edge of the pit. They soared across and landed on the other side.

"Good job," I said, patting them each on the back. "Now let's get out of here."

"Uh oh," said Jonthun. "Look."

Stretched out against the wall, the g'slith g'slythe had started to slither past the pit.

Up, I told the ring. I grabbed the handle on the green door and pushed it down. I held on with both hands. *Back.*

The door opened a sliver.

"No!" screeched Jesska. "Close it."

Through the crack, I saw a wide room filled with dirt. All over the ground were tall mounds that looked as if they had chimneys on top. They reminded me of pictures I'd seen of the giant anthills in Africa. Or were they termite hills?

"Close it. Close it," Jesska cried, bouncing up and down beside me.

"Why?"

"No time to waste," Jesska said. "Hurry."

The fear on Jesska's face scared me.

Forward. The ring pushed the door shut.

"But how will we get out?"

Jesska wasn't listening. She was pushing herself flat against the wall.

I swung around.

The g'slith g'slythe was past the pit and headed for Niklus and Tashee. Their bodies were rigid, and their eyes were wide and staring.

With a jump, I shoved Niklus to the side, and then I took Tashee by the shoulders and shook her.

"Outrageousss!"

"We can't ssstare at ssso many at the sssame time."

"We'll ssstarve."

"Lisssten. I have a sssuggestion."

Hiss. Whisper. Mutter.

"Yesss!"

The k'roll k'pollies, Tashee and I all backed away and braced ourselves for an attack.

"Jesska and I will take care of them," Niklus said.

"Just like before," agreed Jesska.

"And I'll help too," piped Jonthun.

"I don't think it'll work a second time," I told them, "but you can try. Tashee and I will see if we can come up with a more permanent solution."

"All right," said Tashee, "But let's do it from the other side of the pit. I never think well when I'm about to be eaten."

I slipped my arm around Tashee's waist and used the ring to carry us across to the other side. When we looked back, the g'slith g'slythe was crammed into a corner. Its tail was twisted together with the tip tucked under.

Up. Down. Back. Front. Side to Side.

The three k'roll k'pollies bounced and rolled in front of the snake.

The tail slapped Niklus into the wall. When he bounced back, it hit him again.

Whap. Whap. Whappity. Whap.

In a rapid succession of smacks, the snake's tail knocked Niklus into the wall again and again and again. When Jonthun rolled in front and tried to make it stop, he got caught up too. Then Jesska.

Slap. Smack. Strike. Sock.

The snake laughed as it bashed them. One, two, three, into the wall repeatedly.

"Tenderizzze the meat ssso it slidesss easssily into our ssstomach."

"Yum," one head said, "go fassster. I'm ssstarving."

The snake picked up the pace.

Whisk. Whoosh. WONK!

It lost the rhythm.

Niklus, Jesska, and Jonthun bounced off the wall at an angle.

They rolled into the pit and out of sight.

"No!" I shouted.

"No!" screamed Tashee.

"You, ssstupid sssnake," screeched the two heads.

Using the ring, I zipped upward and snatched a torch. Then I grabbed hold of Tashee and leaped into the pit too.

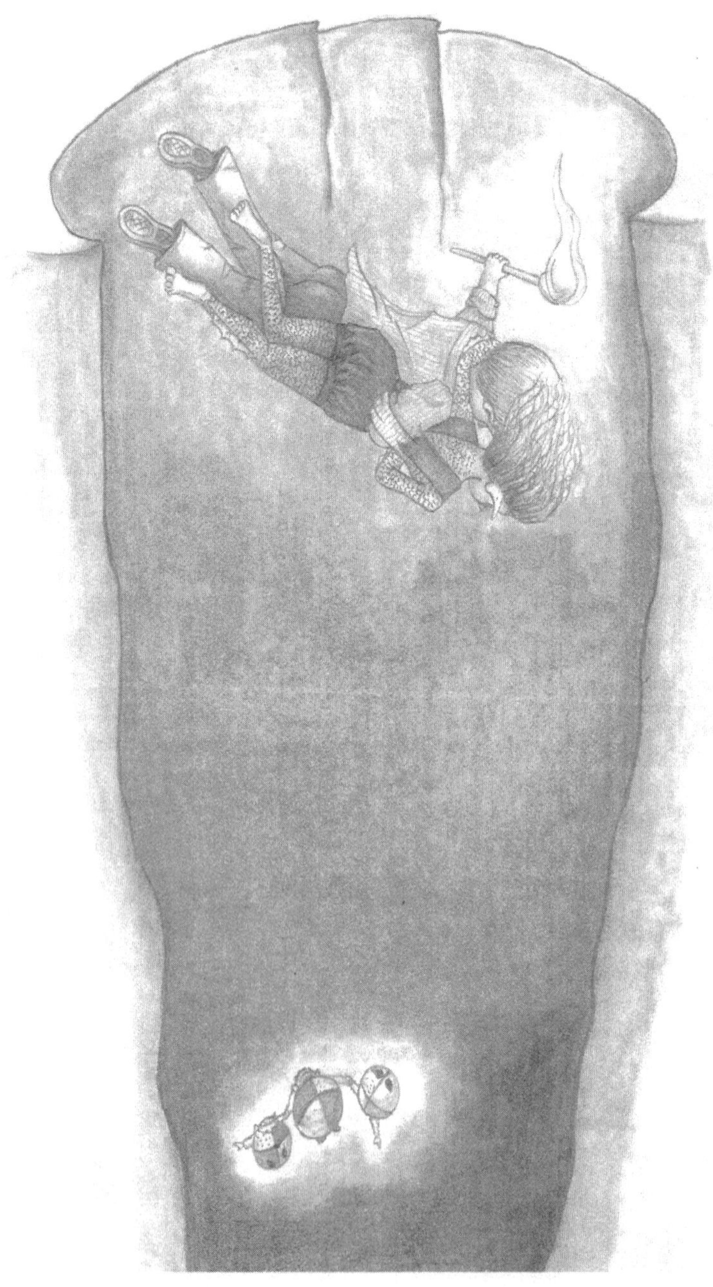

Chapter 23
Down, Down, Down

"What are you doing?" Tashee howled as we fell.

"Saving our friends," I said.

Squinting, I tried to see into the blackness below. Even with the torch, it was like being blind.

Faster, I told the ring.

"Where are they?" I murmured. "Didn't you say the bigger the people, the slower they fall?"

Although I could feel Tashee quivering, her voice sounded perfectly calm. "Yes, but remember Niklus's magic. He can bounce super fast and super high. He can make other people do it too. Maybe he's speeding things up for them all."

"Why would he do that?"

"I don't know. Maybe so they can try bouncing out."

"Nobody can bounce that high," I said.

"I see something," Tashee said.

"Where?" I asked her. *Faster,* I told the ring.

In another few minutes, I saw them too. Jesska's glow gave them a tiny bit of illumination.

Niklus had Jesska and Jonthun by the hand. Every moment, they fell a little faster.

I risked a bit more speed.

"Niklus," I called, "let me help. If Jesska holds onto Jonthun and you grab my foot, I think I can lift you all out."

"Can't" said Niklus. "We're going to see if anyone else is down here. I can help them bounce out. You and Tashee go back up so you don't get in the way."

I was right beside him now. "But—"

"You might let us have the torch," suggested Jesska. "My glow is getting weaker. I've used it too much today."

"All right." After I handed her the torch, I had the ring slow down. Within seconds, the flame looked like a distant star.

I called down after it. "If you aren't topside soon, I'm coming back for you."

"Don't worry," Niklus's faint voice drifted back. "Trust me."

The shadows crowded around, trying to smother me. I looked straight up, and I could see a tiny dot of light. It gave me courage. I told the ring to take us up.

"Do you think the g'slith g'slythe will be waiting for us," Tashee asked.

"Probably. It closed the metal door and there's no handle. It might go out the green door, but Jesska acted like there was something bad on the other side."

"What?"

"She didn't say."

"What'll we do? We can't fight the snake all by ourselves."

"We'll wait for our friends where the g'slith g'slythe can't get us," I assured her.

Zoom. We flew out of the pit and up to the ceiling.

Stop, I told the ring. "We'll wait here."

The snake stretched up on its tails and snapped at us with both heads, but it didn't come close. Then it slunk into a corner and sulked.

"It isss your fault we're ssstuck here."

"You sssaid to ssshut the door."

"Your tail ssslamed it too fassst. I didn't have time to consssider the consssequencesss."

"I hope you ssstarve."

Argue. Bicker. Quarrel.

Talk about fighting with yourself, I thought.

Time passed at a snail's pace.

I have no ideal how long we waited. I had stopped looking at my watch long ago, when I realized that sometimes it went forward and sometimes it went backward.

Plop!

Jesska bounced out of the pit. She was holding hands with a k'roll k'pollie I'd never seen before. He was maroon with reddish fuzz hair.

"Timmy? Tashee?" cried Jesska.

"Up here," I said, lowering us down.

"This is my brother, Chadley," Jesska said. "He—"

Plip. Plop. Two more k'roll k'pollies exploded out of the hole. One was a pale aqua blue girl and the other was a turquoise boy.

"This is Dannee and her twin brother Dannill," Jesska said, introducing the newcomers.

Zoom. Zip. Zap. Jonthun rolled up and out.

Bounce. It was Niklus.

"Six of them," groaned Tashee.

The g'slith g'slythe chortled with glee.

"Sssupper isss ssserved."

"Breakfassst too."

"No ssstarvation today."

"Or any time sssoon."

Then it paused. One head turned to the other. "How can we sssnare so many at onccce?"

"They'll bounccce all over usss."

"Smassshing and crassshing."

"Making usss sssuffer."

"We're not sssafe."

In a panic, the two heads pulled in opposite directions.

"Help usss, Massster."

"Sssave usss."

"You should see down at the bottom," Jonthun said, shivering with excitement. "Slimy stuff on the walls and bones all over the place. It was neat in a gross sort of way."

"Is anyone left down there?" I asked.

"No," Niklus and Jesska answered.

"No k'nick k'nockers?"

The k'roll k'pollies all shook their heads.

“They’re so big, Groklan is afraid to let them in the palace,” Chadley, Jesska’s brother, said. “He keeps them chained together and makes them work outside in the fields.”

“We’ll help them later,” I said. “Right now I have an idea for the g’slith g’slythe.”

Plot. Plan. Propose. Decide.

Laugh. Hoot. Giggle. Snort.

“Shall we do it, team?”

“Yes!” six k’roll k’pollies and one fish-wisher yelled.

“Be sure to watch out for each other,” I said. I used the ring to fetch a torch for Tashee and me. I shouted, “Go team.”

All at once, a whirlwind of k’roll k’pollies bounced, bobbed, swirled, stirred, and rock-and-rolled around the snake.

Instead of trying to catch them, it slunk this way and that.

It tried to wad itself up and hide in the corner.

Sneaking up from behind, Tashee and I jabbed it with our torches.

“Yeeeooowww!” bawled the two heads.

Clobber. Thump. Pummel. Thrash.

K’roll k’pollies battered the snake.

It jerked up and tried to swat them with its tail. It snapped at them with its big mouths. It darted forward, and the k’roll k’pollies jumped back.

Tashee and I crept around, so we got between it and the wall. Then we singed it with our torches again.

Dodge. Slink. Bob. Avoid.

The g’slith g’slythe ducked this way and that, trying to get away from us.

More bouncing. More burning.

The snake spun its heads around in frustration. It wormed away from Tashee and me, getting farther and farther away from the walls.

I winked at Tashee.

Almost there.

I prodded the snake with my torch.

Tashee poked it with hers.

The snake jerked away.

There was nothing left underneath its middle.

The heads yanked forward and the tails shot straight back.

It was too late.

The bulk of the snake's body hung over empty air. It began to droop.

"Ssstupid, ssstupid, ssstupid," one head yelled.

"Don't ssshout at me. It isss your fault."

"Ssshut up." The first head raised itself and butted the second.

That did it.

The rest of the g'slith g'slythe slid over the edge.

"We didn't get sssupper," whined a voice as the snake tumbled end over end.

"Ssserves you right, you ssstupid sssnake."

"Maybe I'll sssnack on you."

"Maybe I'll ssslap you sssilly if you try."

The arguing continued, but I stopped listening.

"Hooray!"

"Whoopee!"

"We did it."

"What do we do now?" Niklus asked.

"Find a way out," I said. "We can't open the metal door because it doesn't have a handle. We can't use the pit because it doesn't go anywhere but down. That only leaves the green door."

"No!" Jesska and the new k'roll k'pollies yelled.

"It's our only choice," I told them. "What's wrong with it? What's in there?"

Jesska trembled when she answered.

"Nip-nappers."

Chapter 24
Big Mouths

"Nip-nappers?" I repeated.

With thumb and forefinger, Niklus made a snapping motion that looked very much like a chomping mouth.

"Nip, nip, nip."

"Maybe they're all asleep," said Chadley. "They were fed earlier this evening."

Gulping, I asked a question even though I didn't want to hear the answer. "Not a person?"

"No," Chadley said. "The soup I made for the guards' dinner was too salty. Groklan ordered it thrown to the nip-nappers and me thrown into the pit."

"Lucky for you it wasn't the other way around," mumbled Tashee.

Jesska touched the boy's maroon arm, as if she couldn't quite believe he'd been rescued. "Chadley is a good cook."

"Was," Chadley corrected with a grin. "I won't ever have to prepare a meal for the g'nome g'nasties again." He glanced around and his smile faded. "Of course, this isn't much of an improvement over the pit."

I asked, "If the nip-nappers are napping, can we sneak past them?"

"I don't think anyone's ever tried," Jesska answered.

"Or if they did—" Dannee started.

"—they didn't live to tell about it," finished Dannill.

"Then I will," I said, sounding braver than I felt. "If they wake up and come after me, I can use the ring to fly out of the way. If they don't, we'll know it's safe."

"No!" Tashee shook her head violently, whipping her bright green hair around like grass in a hurricane. "You're The Chosen One. Your magic stops the g'nome g'nasties. We can't risk losing you."

She tapped her finger on her forehead a moment. "You're also the only one who can open and close the doors. We need someone else to go in there. Someone we can do without if something goes wrong." She looked straight at Niklus.

"Me?" He pulled back with a start, bumping into Jesska, who crashed into Chadley, who knocked Jonthun into Dannee and Dannill.

Bouncing k'roll k'pollies were everywhere.

When the ruckus stopped, Tashee stood with her hands on her hips. "Do you have a better idea?"

Eyes wide, Niklus shook his head.

"I'll go." Everyone stared. Jonthun's tan face was almost white and his lower lip trembled. "It has to be me. If the nip-nappers attack, I can roll up the walls and across the ceiling. If they catch me?" He shrugged. "No big loss. I do everything wrong anyway."

Pulling Jonthun to him, Niklus gave him a hug. "No, Jonthun, I'll go. I can roll faster and bounce way higher than you can."

Frustrated, I started pacing along the wall.

What a mess.

Poor little Jonthun ready to sacrifice himself. There had to be a better way.

I turned to the new k'roll k'pollies.

"What about your magic," I asked. "What can you do?"

Chadley looked down at his feet, a discouraged expression on his face. "I can make things like rocks and furniture roll and bounce wherever I want. But it only works on things that aren't alive. It won't work on nip-nappers."

"I can bounce up and not come down until I want to," Dannill said.

"And I can make people see me when I'm not really there," said Dannee. "It's fun when we're playing tag or other games. I don't see how it will help now."

"This is silly," Tashee said, stamping her foot. "Timmy, use the magic ring to get out. Then you can come around and open that door from the other side." She pointed to the metal one without a handle. "It's the only way to save everyone."

I shook my head. "Too many things can go wrong. Like, I might get lost. Or some g'nome g'nasties might show up while I'm gone. There's no place for you to hide except in the pit, and the g'slith g'slythe is in there."

"I didn't think of that," Tashee said, frowning.

"We have to stick together," I said. "We have a lot of magic among us. Surely we can get past the nip-nappers if we help each other."

One by one, the k'roll k'pollies nodded. Then Tashee did too.

Using the ring to help me, I cracked open the door so I could peer through.

"I don't see any nip-nappers," I whispered. "The door on the other side has a lock. I'll take Tashee across so she can unlock it. When I give you a wave, begin coming over single file. Roll, don't bounce, and be as quiet as possible."

I took hold of the edge of the door with both hands and pulled.

Creak.

I held my breath. No movement from the ant hills.

Again, I pulled.

Squeak. Creak.

I froze.

Still, no nip-nappers.

I gave one more tug.

Creeeeeak!

I waited, watched, and listened. I counted slowly to one hundred. All remained quiet.

"I think it's safe."

When Tashee climbed up on my back, I realized I'd lost track of my backpack ages ago. Thank heavens, I'd put my harmonica in my pocket.

As silent as moonbeams, we glided over the first nip-napper hill. I kept a steady watch every which way. We flew past the second hill, and then the third.

Oh no!

Four insect-like creatures, about the size of my fist, lay in the dirt. They were striped orange and yellow, their legs were folded under them, and their long, narrow heads were tipped forward as if they were asleep.

Dang! I hate bugs. What I wouldn't give right now for a great big can of Raid.

One rolled over and yawned. Its mouth was huge, almost as long as the whole head, and it was full of sharp little teeth.

Tashee gasped.

I nodded to let her know I'd noticed them too. I glanced to the rear to see how far we'd come. About a third of the way. The k'roll k'pollies were lined up ready to start across. Chadley was in front and Niklus was at the end.

With my thumb and forefinger I made the gesture Niklus used to mimic nip-nappers, and then I pointed at them.

I motioned for the k'roll k'pollies to come ahead.

Putting my finger to my lips, I reminded them to be very, very quiet.

I had the ring take Tashee and me to the other door.

She began working on the lock.

As the k'roll k'pollies passed the sleeping bugs, each one of them paused for a quick look.

When Niklus reached them, he smothered a yelp by pressing his hands across his mouth. Keeping his eyes on the nip-nappers, he rolled forward.

Since he wasn't watching where he was going, he bumped into Jonthun, who knocked Dannee into her twin brother, who hit Jesska, who sent Chadley flying.

It was a k'roll k'pollie bounce-fest.

The nip-nappers leaped up and started chittering loudly. I figured they were probably calling all their friends to dinner. A couple dozen poured out of the nearest hill.

Jabbering in clicks and hisses, they all charged at Niklus, who was closest.

Tashee had just finished with the lock.

"Watch out," she shrieked.

"Use your magic," I yelled needlessly.

Jonthun had already rolled up a wall.

Niklus sped around the room, a rolling brown blur.

Five or six images of Dannee bounced in different directions, and Dannill bounced up and didn't come down.

As if they were in the eye of a hurricane, Jesska and Chadley stood quietly in the middle of a swirling mass of dirt and rocks.

"If all k'roll k'pollies have magic like this," I said to Tashee, "why are they afraid of nip-nappers?"

"Because they know they can't keep it up forever. When they run out of energy, the nip-nappers will have them."

"Then we've got to do something." I zoomed into the *pit room* and grabbed a torch off the wall. "Maybe we can herd them with fire like we did the g'slith g'slythe."

"Good idea," Tashee said, taking a torch too.

It didn't help. We waved the flames at the bugs. We jabbed them. I even tried to squash one. Nothing worked. They weren't afraid of fire, they were nonflammable, and their shells were like armor.

Dang!

Scattered here and there among the ant hills were clusters of small rocks. I swooped down and grabbed two handfuls. Flying over the nip-nappers like a dive-bomber, I strafed them with gravel. Rat-a-tat-tat. It didn't hurt them, but they didn't like it.

They ran.

I ducked down for another handful.

"Yip?" Mozart stuck his head out of my pocket.

He leaped to the ground and dashed after the nip-nappers.

"Yip, yip, yip."

"Mozart!" I cried, darting after him. "Come back."

I just knew a nip-napper would gulp him down in one swallow. But Mozart just yipped louder and gave chase.

The nip-nappers scuttled away from him, first going one way and then turning on a dime and going another.

It reminded me of something I'd seen before.

Then I remembered.

On my uncle's farm one time, a neighbor's dog had gotten in the sheep pen. The dog had barked and snapped and chased them, but it never caught or hurt a sheep. It was as if he enjoyed watching them scamper and hop around.

A nip-napper ran up behind Mozart and nipped him. Mozart shook his hind end and a tuft of wool came out in the bug's mouth.

Mozart wasn't hurt a bit.

He charged forward. Every time he got close to a nip-napper, he dipped his head and acted like he was going to bite off its feet. The nip-napper would leap into the air, clacking its jaws angrily.

Mozart seemed to be having the time of his life.

As more bugs poured out of the hills, he yipped and yapped and rounded them up into one great big pack.

All right. Pest control time.

I used the ring to pull the green door open all the way.

"In here, Mozart," I called.

"Yip, yip, yip." Mozart herded them in the right direction.

"Yes," Niklus yelled, quickly catching on to my plan. He slowed himself down until a bunch of nip-nappers took off after him, then he sped up and followed Mozart.

"Yip, yip." Mozart chased his herd straight into the pit. Like a cattle stampede, they couldn't stop.

Stumble. Skid. Slip.

They tumbled over the side.

When Niklus reached the pit, he paused just long enough to give a big bounce, and he sailed up and over. The nip-nappers leaped after him. They didn't make it.

Down, they went.

Right behind Niklus, Jonthun led another batch of bugs. He rolled into the pit, banking like a racer on the lip of the hole. The nip-nappers chasing him disappeared into oblivion.

Then three Dannees, each being chased by a group of nip-nappers, ran over to the pit, but the Dannees vanished and the bugs took the plunge.

Finally, by making a tornado out of swirling sand, Chadley managed to suck up a couple hundred nip-nappers, which he dumped in after the others.

Bugs that tried to escape were gathered up by Mozart.

When the last orange and yellow striped nip-napper had fallen from sight, Mozart yipped happily. He leaped into the air and landed neatly back in my pocket.

Niklus and Jonthun laughed, jumped, and did a belly-slam.

Whoosh! They flew apart, hit the walls, and rebounded into the other k'roll k'pollies, who dribbled all over the place.

"Hooray," shouted Tashee. "Hooray."

"We got rid of them forever," Chadley yelled.

After the celebrating died down, Niklus scuffed his boot across the floor. "I'm sorry I woke up the nip-nappers."

"Don't worry about it," I said, but Tashee interrupted me.

"You may be clumsy, and you may not watch what you're doing sometimes, but no one can say you're not brave. The nip-nappers are gone, and you realized right away how to use your magic to help get rid of them. You did a good job."

Niklus grinned and blushed dark brown.

A very faint voice drifted up from the pit.

"What isss that sssound? Isss it a rain ssshower?"

"In the pit? You ssstupid sssnake, of courssse not."

Raising my eyebrows, I looked around innocently. "The g'slith g'slythe has company. I wonder if they'll get along."

"Sssomething hit me. Are you sssure it'sss not raining?"

"I'm sssure. Hey, sssomething hit me too. It bit me!"

"Me too. Oh no. Nip-nappersss."

"Help. Sssomebody sssave usss."

"Nope," I said. "Guess not."

Laughing, we all headed over to the door that led out.

I pulled it open wide.

Four g'nome g'nasties were just a few feet away.

They gaped at us in surprise.

"That's them," one of the guards shouted. "They're the ones Groklan wants."

"Back," I told my friends.

We dashed into the room we'd just left.

The guards jumped forward and chased us.

"Uh oh," Jonthun cried out. "More nip-nappers."

Chapter 25

Decisions, Decisions

Jerking my head around, I stared.

A couple dozen nip-nappers climbed out of the ant hills in the back of the room. They glanced around, and then took after the k'roll k'pollies.

"Heavy sleepers," Tashee said. "Woke up late."

Without saying anything, we all made the same decision at the same time. We had no intention of taking on the bugs again.

Whish. Dannill and Dannee were a couple of turquoise streaks as they circled around the guards and flew out the door to the hall.

Zip. Zap. Jesska and Chadley rolled right behind them.

Bounce. Bounce. Niklus slammed into the g'nome g'nasties. They fell. He bounced over them and was gone.

The guards scrambled up.

Jump. Spring. Vault. Jonthun knocked them down again on his way to the door.

Swoosh! Tashee and I were out too.

Pressing the ring on the door, I yelled *Forward!*

Blam. The door slammed shut.

Tashee stuck her hand in the lock.

Click. Clack.

Pound. Bang. Slap. Hit.

"Let us out!"

Yell. Shout. Scream. Screech.

"Here they come. Step on them."

"Look out. Behind you."

"Ouch. Ouch. They're fast."

With her lips pursed thoughtfully, Tashee asked me, "Who do you think will win?"

"The guards," I said, giving the door a pat. "There aren't very many nip-nappers left, and the g'nome g'nasties are pretty big."

"Too bad," Tashee said with an exaggerated sigh.

"Where do you want to go from here?" Chadley asked. "We probably shouldn't stay too long in this hallway."

"I need to get back to Prince Seth."

"I'm sorry to have to tell you," Dannee said, "but right before we got tossed into the pit, we heard that the k'nick k'nocker teenies have the sickness now, just like the adults."

"Oh no," I cried. "Prince Seth could be dying."

Tears started oozing down Jesska's face. "The k'roll k'pollie teenies have been sick for almost a week. That's why we've had to do the cooking and cleaning." She waved a hand around. "We're the oldest slaves who can still work."

"We'll catch it next," Dannill said. "Some adults have already died. Then it'll be the teenies. Then us."

"We need a plan," I said. I handed my harmonica to Jonthun. "If you see any g'nome g'nasties, freeze them." Then I sat down cross-legged right there in the hall. "You four have been slaves for a while. Tell me how we can get rid of Groklan."

Plopping down next to me, Tashee said, "I think if we rescued Pink-Dotted Bertie first, she could help."

"But you said wish-fish magic doesn't work against Groklan."

Tashee frowned at me but nodded.

"Maybe we could free the slaves," Chadley said. He sat with his stubby legs straight out in front of him and scratched his head. "If we increased our numbers, we'd be stronger and have more magic to use."

"That won't work," Jesska said. "The adults and teenies are sick. Most of the young ones are too afraid to stand up to Groklan."

"What about the k'nick k'nocker slaves?" I asked. "Could we get them to help?"

"They're in chains and working in the fields," Jesska said. "It would take forever to round them up."

Dannee stared at her hands and her voice was barely a whisper. "Maybe we could break Groklan's magic mirror. I was cleaning his room a few weeks ago, and I heard him and Ugor talking. It's the mirror that causes the sickness, and hides the sun, and makes the wish-fish magic not work. It also makes it so no new babies can be born."

"One time when I was taking Groklan his dinner," Dannill said, "I heard Ugor say a mirror crowned Groklan king by making him so big and strong. Maybe it's the same mirror."

"Do either of you know where he keeps it?"

Dannee and Dannill shook their heads.

"I've looked and looked," Dannee said, "whenever I've been assigned to clean. I've searched his whole bedroom. There's one mirror on the wall, but I don't think it's the one. Groklan hardly glances at it, and it doesn't feel magical to me."

"If I was Groklan," I said, "I'd keep it in the throne room. That's where his books of magic are, and that's where he makes decisions and tells other people what to do. It's where he's the most powerful."

"I'd keep it on me," said Jesska.

"Unless it was too big to carry," Chadley pointed out.

"Does anyone know what it looks like?"

The k'roll k'pollies shook their heads.

Tashee jumped to her feet and began pacing around in a circle. "Anything that reflects a picture can be called a mirror," she said. "It could even be the buttons on his shirt or his belt buckle."

"Not Groklan's buttons," Jesska said. "They're made of bone, and most of his belt buckles are covered with leather. I noticed when I had to do his laundry."

"What about a jewel?" Chadley suggested. "He might wear a ring or a pendant."

"That's possible," I said, "but we'd have to get pretty close to him to check it out. Maybe we could save it for last. Where do you think we should start? Dannee has already done his bedroom."

"I like your idea about the throne room," said Tashee, leaning against the wall. "If we don't find it there, the next place I'd look would be Ugor's bedroom. I'll bet he doesn't get many visitors, which means anything hidden in there would be pretty safe."

"I've looked around the throne room a little," Dannee said, "when I've been dusting. He has dozens of mirrors in there."

"Maybe he has a spell on it to hide it," Jesska said. "He's a wizard. When he decided to have k'roll k'pollie slaves, he might have hidden his important things from us with spells."

"Fish-wishers are very sensitive to magic," Tashee said. "I think I could spot a spell, even a hiding spell, if I was close enough."

"At least we won't have to watch out for g'nome g'nasties while we search," Niklus said, pointing at the harmonica in Jonthun's hand. "We have Timmy's magic to take care of them."

"I vote for starting in the throne room," Chadley said, bouncing to his feet. "Come on. I know a shortcut."

Halfway down the hall, he popped open a secret panel in the wall. There were stairs inside, going up and down.

I looked at Jesska. "These are like the tunnels you helped us escape through, aren't they? Are they all over the place?"

"Yes," Chadley answered for his sister. When we were all crowded together on a little landing, he closed the panel. He motioned us upward.

As we climbed, Chadley continued talking. "Hundreds and hundreds of years ago, Shalamar only had one king and this was his palace. There were little people called elves who served the k'whish k'wise king. They could move really fast, and these were their tunnels. They used them to run errands and deliver messages."

My foot slipped, and I grabbed the wall for support. "K'whish k'wise? Nobody told me about them. Where are they now?"

"The k'whish k'wise disappeared a long time ago," Dannee said.

"No one knows where they went or why," added Dannill.

"They were scholars and seers," Jesska said. "Some people think they saw something terrible in the future, and it frightened them enough that they ran away and hid."

"Flew away," Niklus corrected with a little laugh. "They had wings and made a whishing sound when they flew. That's how they got their name."

"How do you know so much about them if they disappeared so long ago?" I asked.

We reached another landing and started up the next flight of stairs.

"We study them in school," Jonthun said. "I hate history."

I was in the middle of a step, and I stopped, foot still in the air. "You go to school?"

"Of course," everyone answered, including Tashee.

"We did," said Dannee, "until Groklan made us slaves."

A great dismay settled over the k'roll k'pollies.

"Yesterday was Grindlemach Day," said Chadley sadly. "No presents this year."

"Not one single wham k'bam pie either," grumbled Niklus.

Jonthun began to sniffle. "Our mom was going to bake the first one of the season when the g'nome g'nasties came."

"Chadley and I were gathering jolly-holly," said Jesska, "to decorate the house when we were caught."

The mood became very somber, and everyone climbed the stairs with heavy feet. I felt awful. I had been focused on Prince Seth because he was my ticket home. I hadn't looked at the situation from the k'roll k'pollies point of view.

Actually, because they were sort of silly looking, I hadn't quite taken them seriously. Now I realized their whole lives had been turned upside down too. They were separated from their families, torn away from their homes. Happy times had been disrupted and their traditions ruined. Plus they had the added fear and humiliation of being slaves to the g'nome g'nasties.

"The strangest thing about the k'whish k'wise," Dannill said, "was that they were all one color and one shade."

"Gold," said Jesska. Suddenly, she giggled and the sad mood was broken. "Can you imagine anything more absurd than having everyone look exactly the same?"

"How could you tell each other apart?" said Niklus.

The k'roll k'pollies all laughed.

In a high squeaky voice, Jonthun said, "May I present my son, who is gold. And this is my daughter, who is also gold."

"Or is it the other way around?" Niklus said.

More giggles and chuckles.

It was so contagious, even Tashee and I were laughing.

One nice thing about k'roll k'pollies, I thought, *they're basically cheerful. They don't stay depressed long.*

We came to another landing and Chadley told us to wait there.

"This is the tricky part," he whispered. He opened another secret door, which was behind a towering stone statue. He pointed down a long corridor. "We go down the hall, turn the corner, go down another corridor—"

"Shhh." I pressed a finger to my lips, cocked my head to the side, and listened. "Footsteps."

Chapter 26

Daring Deeds Done

While the others stayed put, I poked my head around the statue. "Six guards."

"Leave them to me," said Dannee. "I'll lure them over there."

Across from us and down a ways was an open door with a key hanging beside it on a hook.

Suddenly, the image of Dannee appeared in the middle of the hall. "Oh no! Guards. How can I get away? What'll I do?"

"Get her," a voice yelled.

Thud. Thud. Thud.

Loud feet pounded the floor.

The guards didn't even notice the rest of us, crowded behind the statue, watching.

The fake Dannee looked all around, as if she were too panic-stricken to decide which way to go. When the guards were almost to her, she turned and dashed through the open door. They were right behind her.

Zoom! I used the ring to take me there. I grabbed the key off the hook, slammed the door and locked it.

"Where'd the k'roll k'pollie go?" a guard yelled.

"Who closed the door?" shouted another.

Shake. Rattle. Jiggle.

"The door's stuck."

"Let's find that k'roll k'pollie first. She has no business in this corridor. She must be a runaway."

"Maybe she's hiding behind those chests."

"I love doing that," Dannee said. "Everyone gets so confused when my image disappears."

"Good job," I told her. "Lead the way, Chadley."

"We have to go right by the guards' dining room, so let's be real quiet," he said.

As we turned the corner, I realized I still had the key in my hand. I was just about to levitate and put it back, when Tashee took it from me.

"It might get lost. I'd better put it in a safe place." She stuck it in her pocket. "Can't be any safer than that."

All along the hallway were huge stone statues of Groklan. They were so tall they almost reached the high ceiling. Between them were windows with red drapes held back by golden cords. Outside the sky was roiling with dark, threatening storm clouds.

We came to two wide doors on the left.

"Dining room," Chadley whispered.

Tashee and I tiptoed forward. The others rolled.

Through the closed doors, the clatter of plates and silverware blended with many voices that were talking and laughing and arguing. It sounded just like the cafeteria at school. I was surprised to find I missed being there.

More disturbing than the sounds, though, were the smells. I was on a foreign planet, but I recognized the scent of warm bread, fried meat, and fresh-sliced fruit.

"Dinner," Niklus murmured. He licked his lips and rubbed his belly. "I'm very, very hungry."

"Me too," said the others.

Me too, I thought. "After we destroy the magic mirror, we'll find something to eat. I promise."

I was ready to move on, but I noticed Chadley studying one of the images of Groklan. He grinned at Jesska and she nodded. They joined hands. The statue started to rock on its base.

Gasping, I took a couple of steps back.

The statue tipped over.

I expected it to land with a terrible crash, probably shattering and spraying us with rock slivers that would slice us to pieces.

Instead, the stone Groklan drifted to the floor as silently as a falling leaf.

"Did you do that?" I asked Chadley.

"Me and Jesska," He said. "I can't lift things that heavy by myself."

"I thought Jesska's magic was making light," I said.

"It is," Jesska told me. "I can create a light, and I can make things light."

I shook my head, puzzled.

She smiled brightly. "Light has two meanings. I can make a glowing light, and I can make heavy things light in weight. I made the statue lighter so Chadley could move it."

"Ah," I said, finally getting it. "Light and *light*."

"Right."

"But why make the statue light and move it?"

"We might as well keep this bunch of guards from causing trouble," Chadley said. He wiggled his fingers, and the statue rolled right up to the doors and stopped.

Hmmm, the doors seemed to be hung backward. At home doors opened inward. Here they all seemed to open out.

Jesska pointed at it, and it settled down hard. "No one's coming through there for a while."

"Back door?" I asked.

Chadley shook his head. "Only other way out is through a window, and we're three stories up."

"What about the kitchen?"

"The kitchen is down below. The food is lifted using a big dumbwaiter."

"Neat trick," Tashee said. She ran her hand along the stone. "Someday when you're not busy, maybe you'd move my rock to a cooler part of the swamp."

Jesska and Chadley both said, "Sure."

"What do we do after we get down this hall," I asked.

"Turn left. Then it's only a little ways to another secret panel. Behind it are more stairs, but once we get to the top of those, we'll be right behind Groklan's throne."

We were so busy watching Chadley move the statue and trap the g'nome g'nasties, we didn't even hear the ones who marched around the corner and almost trampled us.

In the time it took Jonthun to get the harmonica to his lips, the guards charged at us.

One guard almost grabbed Tashee by the hair. She ducked and whirled around, shouting, "Don't you dare touch me." He was so surprised he dropped his hand and gawked.

After that, he couldn't have touched her anyway. Jonthun blew into the harmonica. All the g'nome g'nasties froze.

Jumping up, Tashee tried to slap the guard's hand. She couldn't reach it, so she smacked his leg instead. "I've always wanted to hit a g'nome g'nasty," she said. "I think I'll do it again." Whap! "Wow, that felt good." Whap. Whap. Whap. "Too bad I'm not strong enough to do some real damage."

She gave me an idea.

"Hey," I said, "do any of you know where we can get some rope?"

"Rope?" asked Niklus.

"Might as well keep these guards from bothering us too."

The others started to smile, but when Dannill spoke up, the smiles faded.

"No rope around here. All the supply rooms are on the other side of the castle. All that's up here are ones like where Dannee lured the guards. They're linen closets."

"Dang it."

"How about the cords from the drapes?" Jesska suggested. "There's plenty."

"Excellent," I said. "Chadley and Dannill, why don't you help Jesska get the cords? Niklus and Dannee, you can help me with an old Earth trick."

"What do you want us to do?" Niklus asked.

"I'll show you." I went over to the nearest guard's boot. Unlike k'nick k'nockers and k'roll k'pollies, who wore boots that pulled on, the g'nome g'nasties wore ones that laced and tied.

Yanking hard, I pulled a bowknot apart. "Untie their boots, and then tie the strings to the boots of someone else. Be sure you make a square knot." I showed them how.

Up and down the hall, we went, untying and retying shoelaces.

When Chadley, Jesska, and Dannill hauled over a pile of cords, I went to help them. We wrapped cord around arms and legs, looped it through belts, and wove it in and out among the guards. We tied the ends together at random. Soon, they looked as if they had been caught in a gigantic spider's web.

The more we did, the more we chuckled.

By the time all the cord was gone and all the boots were tied together, we were about doubled over from laughing so hard.

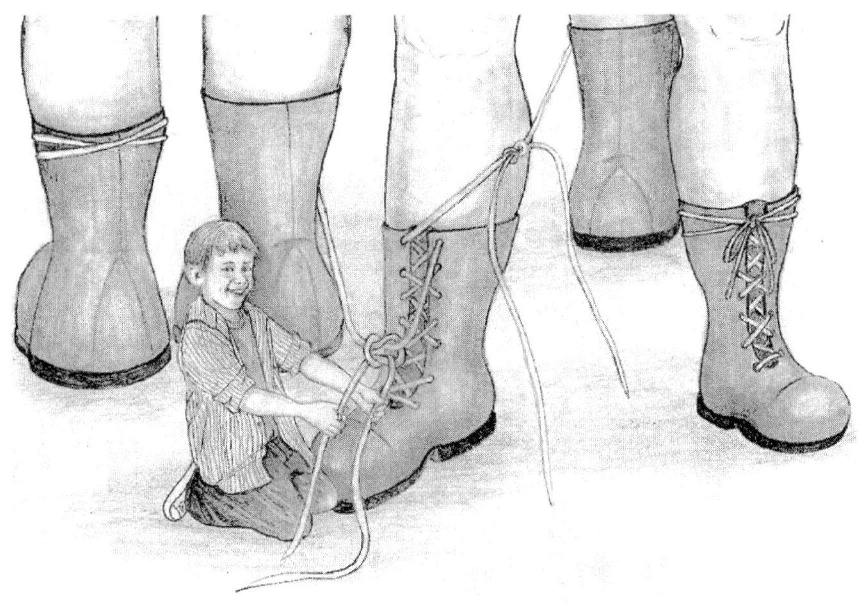

I didn't realize Jonthun was laughing instead of blowing on the harmonica until the g'nome g'nasties began thrashing around. They tripped over their feet and pulled each other down onto the floor in a big mountain of bumbling bodies.

K'roll k'pollies bounced and rolled to keep from being crushed in the confusion. I seized Tashee and zipped out of the way.

A thunderous voice roared from the end of the hall.

"WHAT IS GOING ON HERE?"

Chapter 27

A Tack on the Throne

There at the end of the hall, with his hands on his hips and his red eyes blazing, was Groklan.

"Run," I screamed. "Uh no. Roll. Bounce. Something."

Tashee slapped my face, just like they do in the movies when someone is hysterical.

"Flee," she yelled.

There were g'nome g'nasties all over the floor.

When the k'roll k'pollies bounced, they landed on heads, stomachs, backs, arms, and legs.

Umph. Ouch. Ugggh. Yeow.

"This way," shouted Chadley.

We didn't dawdle. We rushed to follow him.

Groklan plunged after us.

"Get out of my way, fools," he roared at the guards.

Thud. Smack. Punch. Kick.

The guards howled and cursed as they tried to untangle themselves and get out of Groklan's way.

With no regard for his men, Groklan plowed right over them.

We darted around a corner.

Chadley pushed on a design curved in a stone. A section of wall slid open.

Whoosh. Zip. Zap. Zoom. We whipped through the opening.

Flash. Bam. Chadley closed it behind us.

“When Groklan gets past the guards and can’t see us running away,” I said, “won’t he guess we ducked in here?”

“I doubt it,” Chadley answered. “The tunnels are too small for g’nome g’nasties. He probably doesn’t even know they’re here.”

“He might,” said Jesska. “The g’slith g’slythe liked to hunt runaway slaves in the tunnels. He might have told Groklan about them.”

“Then he’d better see us,” Dannee said with a grin, “or at least one of us.” She patted herself on the chest.

“You mean you’re going to stay behind?” I asked.

“No. I’ll just send an image of me down the hall.” She pressed her ear to the wall. “Here he comes.” She flicked her fingers. “There goes Dannee.”

“I see you, k’roll k’pollie,” roared Groklan as he ran past us outside the panel.

Sizzle. Crackle.

BOOM!

Dannee’s eyes flew open wide and she shivered. “He must have shot his fright-lightning at me. Whew. I’m glad that’s not really me out there.”

Making a shooing motion with his hands, Chadley soon had us clomping up stairs again. We followed the tunnel through a couple of turns to another secret door.

We stepped through and were behind Groklan’s huge black throne.

“Let’s find that magic mirror,” Dannill said enthusiastically.

“Just a minute.” I had something to say, but I wasn’t exactly sure how to put it. I didn’t want to hurt anyone’s feelings. I bit my lip for a moment and then blurted it out. “We have to do more than find the mirror.”

“Of course,” said Tashee. “We have to find Pink-Dotted Bertie, and the other wish-fish, whoever he is.”

“That’s not what I meant.” I motioned for Jonthun to hand me the harmonica. I held it up. “This magic isn’t really too useful.”

“Did you crack open your head or something?” demanded Tashee. “Paralyzing g’nome g’nasties isn’t useful?”

“It’s temporary,” I said. “When the music stops, the g’nome

g'nasties don't even know they've been stopped. They just go on doing whatever they were doing before."

"Yes but—" Chadley stopped in the middle of his sentence. "You're right. It doesn't change anything."

"On Earth people like the g'nome g'nasties are called bullies. That's what Groklan is, a great big bully."

"So?" Niklus said. "What can we do?"

"Sometimes, you have to fight back."

"F-f-f-f-fight Groklan," Jonthun stammered. "No way."

"Why not?" I asked. "We fought the nip-nappers and won. We fought the g'slith g'slythe and won. Why not the g'nome g'nasties?"

Dannill chewed on his lip nervously. "They're so big, and we're so small."

"You heard the fright-lightning," Dannee said. "Groklan has powerful magic."

"So do we," I said, "especially when we work together."

Heads moved from side to side. Mouths shaped the word *no*.

Holding up the harmonica again, I told them, "Remember, if all else fails, I can freeze them. But we have to come up with a permanent solution before everyone dies."

No one looked at anyone else.

I think they were embarrassed to admit how afraid they were.

I was frightened too. I just didn't see any other options.

Then Niklus bounced once and stood beside me. "I'm really good at knocking people over. I can knock over g'nome g'nasties."

After a second, Chadley bounced to my other side. "I'm tired of being a slave. I can roll things into them. If Jesska helps, I can roll really heavy things on top of them."

Jesska slid next to her brother. "I'll help. I might be able to blind them with shots of light too. If I can't, I'll throw things."

With her lips trembling, Dannee bounced next to Jesska. "I can confuse them and make them run around in circles."

"All right," Dannill said, "I'll float in the air and drop things on their heads."

Jonthun rolled over to Niklus, but he looked sad. "I'm not sure how my magic can help."

"Don't worry," said Niklus. "You can do lots of stuff. You're small enough to get between their feet and make them trip. You can roll up the walls and throw things at them like Jesska."

"You can spit on them from the ceiling," Tashee muttered, shaking her head at our foolishness.

"Yeah." Jonthun's eyes grew bright with anticipation. "I've got lots of spit. And k'roll k'pollie spit is really disgusting."

"You're all crazy," Tashee said. She pointed her finger at me accusingly, "And you, Mister Timothy Alan Parker Earthling Human, are the craziest of all. Do you think you and six k'roll k'pollies can fight g'nome g'nasties and win? Our parents didn't win. The kings didn't win. The wish-fish didn't win."

I stood tall. "All we can do is try! Somebody has to teach them that people don't like being pushed around."

"Us!" shouted the k'roll k'pollies.

"Besides," I said solemnly, "what do we have to lose? Everyone in the world is going to die if we don't get the sun back and stop the illness from spreading."

"All right," Tashee grumbled. "You fight. I'll look for the wish-fish and the magic mirror."

"Fair enough," I said. "You search while we put a tack on Groklan's chair."

"A tack?"

"Never mind," I said. "It's just another way of saying we're going to booby-trap this room."

"Booby-trap?"

When I explained, the k'roll k'pollies immediately got into the spirit and started thinking of things they could do.

Tashee stomped off. She climbed a bookcase and stroked an oval mirror hanging on the wall. "No magic here," she said.

She started to climb down then looked in the mirror again. "Oh dear, my hair is a mess." She raked her fingers through it, making it stand up more, patted the sides, and moved on.

Soon everyone was busy.

Jesska toured the room, making heavy objects lighter so the others could maneuver them.

Dannill floated up and balanced a pitcher of water on top of a door that was opened a crack.

"I know what to do with this." Niklus held a jar full of brightly colored balls. "It's glob-rock candy." He and Jonthun spread them on the floor in front of all the doors.

"Great." I gave them a thumbs-up.

Niklus picked up a glob-rock and stuck it into his mouth.

He went to help Dannee and Dannill.

She pulled cords from all the drapes. He hovered in the air and tied the ends to a chandelier that hung in the middle of the room. They tied the other ends around some big glass vases. Then they pulled the vases back and tied them with slip knots to the candle sconces on the wall.

Jonthun gathered a bunch of knickknacks and books, which he piled on the lintels that jutted out above the windows.

Jesska and Chadley moved several statues to spots where they could roll without smashing into anything except g'nome g'nasties.

Then Jesska twitched her fingers and everything returned to its normal weight.

Standing in the middle of the room, I looked around. We were ready. Just like in *Home Alone.*

"Let's all help Tashee look for the mirror. There's no telling how long it'll take before someone thinks to look for us here."

"You don't need to worry about Groklan," Dannee said. "He's still chasing my image around the other floor. When you're ready for him, let me know. I'll lead him here."

"Excellent," I said. "If you see something and you can't tell if it is magical or not, tell Tashee so she can take a look at it."

We searched.

There were big mirrors hanging on the walls, and small ones lying on tables and bookcases. Tiny ones decorated figurines and bric-a-brac. After Tashee checked them all, we started looking for other things that were shiny.

"Nothing," Tashee said gloomily. "Maybe it's not in here after all. Maybe we'd better start looking somewhere else."

"Dang," I said. "Well, finding the mirror was only half the plan. The other part was standing up to Groklan. If we capture him, maybe we can force him to tell us where it is."

"Capture him?" gulped Niklus. "You never said anything about capturing him."

"What would we do with him?" asked Jesska.

"You wouldn't kill him, would you?" asked Dannee.

My mouth went dry, and I swallowed hard. I don't even like stepping on spiders.

"No," I said. "But we could lock him up in his own dungeon while we go get Prince Seth."

"If he's not already sick," said Chadley.

"Aren't any of the adults still healthy?" I asked.

The k'roll k'pollies shook their heads.

"If you manage to capture Groklan," Tashee said, "through dumb blind luck, I'll go get His Majesty, All-White Paterick. The wish-fish aren't sick. The High Fin usually doesn't leave the swamp, but his magic is strong enough that he can if he wants. He'll know what to do."

"All right," I said. "We might as well do it." I gave Dannee a nod. "Let's get Groklan up here."

When the k'roll k'pollies were all hidden behind chairs and drapes, I lifted Tashee and put her on a high shelf in one of the bookcases. "You'll be safe here."

I floated near the ceiling.

Thump. Thump. Thump, thump, thump, thump, thump.

Even though everyone could hear what I was hearing, I called out anyway, "He's coming."

Chapter 28
Mirror, Mirror

Wham! The door flew open.

Groklan rushed in.

Ugor was at his heels.

Splat!

Groklan slipped on glob-rocks and fell, sliding clear across the floor and crashing into the base of his throne.

Splash!

The pitcher of water fell on Ugor. It shattered on his hard head and drenched him at the same time. Staggering around, he stepped on a glob-rock and—whap—he hit the floor.

Two, four, six, eight, ten guards poured into the room.

Slip. Slide. Skid.

Down they went.

Seething with fury, Groklan clambered to his feet.

His scum-pond green face glared at me and the k'roll k'pollies with blistering hatred. His red eyes burned like bonfires on a dark night.

Dannee bounced out from behind a chair and stuck out her tongue.

"Ah ha," roared Groklan. He chanted a few words and pointed his finger. A bolt of fright-lightning shot from the tip.

Sizzle. Crack. BOOM.

The lightning went right through the false Dannee and blew up a table.

"Aaaaack," screamed Groklan. "Guards, find them."

The room exploded with k'roll k'pollies.

The guards stood in the middle of the floor, puzzled into immobility, as five Dannees bounced around them.

Whoosh. Niklus swooped out from behind a drape and bowled them over.

When they got back to their feet—clang, bang—Chadley and Jesska rolled a bronze statue in their way, tripping them again.

Not wanting to miss out on the fun, I pulled a slip knot.

Swang. A vase slammed into a guard and shattered.

Swing. Swang. Two more vases smacked two more heads.

Dannill jumped up, bounced, and hovered at the top of a window.

Smash. Crash. He heaved bric-a-brac at the guards so fast, they covered their heads and dashed here and there, trying to keep from getting hit.

"Here's one," a guard yelled as he lunged for Jonthun.

Zoom. Jonthun rolled up the wall, spraying down gobs of blue spit. The guard tried to wipe off the gooey mess and stumbled backward. He stepped on a glob-rock.

Wham. He fell.

"A fish-wisher!" A g'nome g'nasty whooped when he noticed Tashee on the shelf. He lurched that way, dodging glob-rocks and the flying knickknacks Dannill was throwing.

Tashee chucked a book at him. He ducked and kept on coming. She threw another and another.

The guard shrieked and covered his face with his hands. Jesska had used the big mirror on the wall to aim a beam of light straight into his eyes.

Grabbing hold of the very top of the bookcase, Tashee pulled herself up. Then waved her thanks to Jesska and pressed her back against the wall.

A different guard pulled a chair over. He stood on it and reached for her.

No way, Jose, I thought.

Swoosh. I ripped a drape from the window and tossed it over the guard's head. Flapping his arms, he tried to fling it away, but he lost his footing.

Crack. His head hit the floor.

"Are you all right?" I called to Tashee.

She nodded, but she had a strange look on her face. She crooked her finger at me in a *come here* gesture.

"Why would anyone keep water on top of a bookcase?" she asked me. She pointed to a clear glass bowl filled with liquid.

"GET AWAY FROM THERE," yowled Groklan.

Startled, I whipped my head around.

Groklan was staring straight at Tashee and me.

He began chanting, and his finger glowed as he raised his hand.

He's going to blast us! I pulled my harmonica out and began blowing a tune.

All the g'nome g'nasties froze.

As I played, I glanced down and saw my face reflected in the water. I watched my eyes bug out when I realized what I was looking at. *A mirror!*

I looked questioningly at Tashee.

Dipping her hand in the bowl, she delicately swished her fingers around.

My reflection disappeared, and other ones wavered on the surface around the outer edge of the bowl. A sun. Infant k'nick k'nockers and k'roll k'pollies. The eggs of wish-fish and fish-wishers. A greenish fog that washed over people and made them sick. Two fish.

One of the fish was absolutely beautiful. She had a long flowing tail and lacy fins. She was pale pink with hot pink polka dots. The other was pure white except for a tiny amount of silver-gray around his mouth and eyes. A long, spiky fin ran down the whole length of his back.

"It's Pink-dotted Bertie and His Majesty Paterick," breathed Tashee reverently.

In the middle of the bowl was the image of a stubby, squashed-looking g'nome g'nasty. He had a lopsided, ugly head and a bitter, down-turned mouth.

"This is it," Tashee said. "This is Groklan's magic mirror. I'm going to smash it."

She hit it. She kicked it. Nothing happened.

She put her shoulder against it and tried to topple it off the edge of the bookcase.

Scrape. It moved a fraction of an inch.

"Help me," she said.

Still blowing into the harmonica, I scooted around to the back of the bowl.

When Tashee said *go,* I pushed.

Scrip. Scrape.

Dang. It's heavier than it looks. Oh, I know what to do.

I held the harmonica in my left hand, and pressed my right hand against the bowl.

Forward.

Ring, I said FORWARD.

I gave Tashee a bewildered look.

"It is absolutely swarming with spells," she said. "Maybe you can't use magic against it. But it moved when we pushed. We'll just have to push harder."

Again, I tried to shove and blow at the same time.

I couldn't do it very well. I needed to huff and puff from exertion, which made playing the harmonica difficult.

I looked around for Jonthun and Niklus, but they were busy helping Chadley and the others tie up the guards.

"Groklan's moving," screeched Tashee.

In slow-motion Groklan shifted position.

His mouth twitched.

His hand with its glowing finger inched upward.

"He's breaking out of the music magic," Tashee cried.

I've got to choose. Play the harmonica hard enough to keep Groklan frozen or drop it and help Tashee.

It only took me a moment to decide.

I let the harmonica fall.

Hooking my shoulder under the lip of the bowl, I strained with every muscle in my body.

Push. Shove. Drive. Force. Propel.

The bowl flipped over the edge of the bookcase.

"Incoming," I yelled.

Niklus glanced up. "Duck, everyone," he shouted.

"NOOOOOOO!" Groklan's deep voice faded into a high pitched whimper.

Chapter 29

Celebration Time

Crash. Bang.
The glass bowl shattered into a thousand pieces.
Water splashed across the floor.
My eyes fastened onto Groklan.
His body glowed.
He seemed to swell to twice his size. Then he began to shrink.

The glow-in-the-dark red eyes faded to yellow.

The tree-trunk arms and legs shriveled into twigs.

He got shorter and shorter and shorter.

Soon, all that was left of the huge green giant was the ugly little g'nome g'nasty we had seen reflected in the magic mirror.

"You ruined everything," Groklan screamed. Then he sat down on the floor and started to cry.

The guards just stared, then they began squirming and twisting and pulling on the cords that held them.

Ugor climbed from beneath a pile of books, rushed over to Groklan, and put his arms around the tiny giant.

"I'm king," Groklan squealed. "Call out the guards. Surround the palace." He pointed at me and Tashee. "Make them fix my magic mirror. Then, throw them in the pit. Don't let them escape."

"There, there," Ugor said, patting Groklan on the back. "It'll be all right."

Suddenly, a beam of sunlight burst through the clouds and spilled through the window.

"The spell is broken," whooped the k'roll k'pollies. They bounced with joy and rolled around in circles.

"No," Groklan cried. "It's not fair. I studied the magic books. I made the magic mirror. I did all the work. Now the adults will get their magic back, and the sickness will go away, and new babies will be born."

He lay on the floor, kicking and screaming like a two-year old.

"I want to be king. I want all the magic. It's not fair. It's not fair. It's not fair."

"You really are The Chosen One," Tashee said, taking my hand in hers. "I had to tell the k'roll k'pollies that to keep them in line, but I wasn't really quite sure." She gave me a big smile and batted her eyelids at me. "You're cute, too, in a non-fishy, human sort of way."

"Hey, look," Jonthun called. "Someone's coming."

Outside, I saw four flying objects zooming through the air. One was in front, and the others formed a triangle behind it.

A big purple figure waved.

It can't be.

It was.

Swoosh!

Prince Seth and his friends, riding on magic carpets, flew in

through the window, which opened all by itself.

Seth jumped down and looked around the room.

He leaped over the g'nome g'nasties and k'roll k'pollies and ran over to the bookcase where Tashee and I were.

"As soon as I saw the sunlight, I knew you'd won. Jenfer used her magic to show me your adventures until this morning when she got the sickness."

K'roll k'pollies were bouncing all around the prince's feet, so I introduced everyone. He scooped us up in handfuls and set us on a table so we could talk without anyone getting trampled.

"You not only found a fish-wisher," Seth said, "but several other friends as well."

"They're the best," I said. "They're all clever and brave. I couldn't have accomplished anything without them."

"Cute and honest," Tashee said to no one in particular.

"Where's Groklan?" Prince Seth asked.

I pointed at the shrunken giant. "He put himself under a spell. That's what he really is."

As if he didn't believe me, Seth raised a single eyebrow, like a purple Mr. Spock.

Tashee and the k'roll k'pollies all chimed in, saying "It's true."

"We watched him change," Tashee said. "He was big and strong and mean before. Now he's puny and miserable."

"Bilbur and Darrl," Seth called, "tie him up and take him to my father. The kings and The High Fin will decide what to do with him."

Bilbur, the tall green k'nick k'nocker with buzzed quills, grabbed a piece of cord from the floor. Darrl, the yellow one with dimples, reached for Groklan.

Blubbering like a baby, Groklan clutched onto Ugor's arm. "I'm king. Don't let them take me away. Lock them up in the dungeon. Feed them to the nip-nappers."

"I'll go with you, Master." Ugor took off his vest and wrapped it around the tiny, former king. He looked at Prince Seth. "You don't need to bind him. We'll go quietly."

"You'd better," Seth said. Darrl and Bilbur loaded the two g'nome g'nasties on a carpet and flew away.

When they were gone, Seth told me, "You and your friends are all invited to the k'nick k'nocker palace. The cooks are preparing a feast to celebrate your victory."

"Aren't the adults sick?" I asked.

"Not anymore. As soon as you broke the spell, the sickness disappeared." He snapped his fingers. "Just like that."

I poked Niklus with my elbow. "See. I told you we'd get something to eat after we broke the magic mirror."

With his eyes downcast, Niklus scuffed the table top with his foot. "I guess I'm not hungry anymore."

"Not hungry?" I exclaimed. "What's wrong?"

Niklus wiped a tear from his cheek. "We need to find our mom and dad. At first, when I knew it was hopeless, I made myself not think about them. But now? We don't even know if they're still alive."

Nodding, Jonthun took Niklus's hand. "I couldn't enjoy a feast if our baby sister was hungry. We have to go look for them."

“Shandee,” Prince Seth called to the orange k’nick k’nocker who wore dangly earrings. “You can find things with your magic. If they describe their parents and sister, can you find them?”

“Sure,” Shandee said. “Just tell me their names and colors.”

Bouncing with excitement, Niklus said, “Our mom’s name is Ruthleen. She’s pink with yellow curls, and she’s beautiful. Baby Ceeann is rose colored, and she’s just learned to bounce.”

Jonthun pushed Niklus aside. “Our dad’s name is Merlinion. He’s mahogany brown and bald on top. He has just a little blue fuzz by his ears.

“I’ll find them,” said Shandee.

“Bring them to the palace.” Shandee headed for the door, but Seth called her back. “You need to find all the slaves, k’nick k’nocker and k’roll k’pollie. They all deserve a good meal. We’ll have Grindlemach Day late this year.”

“Hooray,” everyone cheered.

“Tashee,” Jesska said softly, “I have something for you.”

Spinning around, Tashee gasped.

Cradled in Jesska’s arm was a glass bowl with green things growing at the bottom. Swimming in the water was Pink-Dotted Bertie.

Tashee glowed with happiness. She dipped her hand in the water. The wish-fish rubbed against her fingers. From within the plants, stately and dignified, The High Fin swam out and greeted Tashee by touching her hand with his nose.

“Oh thank you, Jesska,” Tashee said. Then she jerked around as if she had just had an idea.

“Prince Seth, you don’t need to have your friends search for the slaves. In the very beginning, Timmy told me you were the one who wanted a wish. If you’d like, I’ll ask Pink-Dotted Bertie and His Majesty Paterick to send us all to your castle. The slaves, your friends, everyone except g’nome g’nasties.”

“That would be very kind, if you please.”

POOF!

We were there.

We were all crowded together in an enormous room. There were k’nick k’nockers, k’roll k’pollies, a few fish-wishers, and my friends and I.

“Niklus! Jonthun!” Their mother bounced over a dozen people to reach them. She held a little k'roll k'pollie in her arms, baby Ceeann. Right behind, hopped the biggest k'roll k'pollie I'd ever seen.

"Mom! Dad!" In a flash, they all rolled together, bouncing and hugging and kissing.

Soon, Jesska and Chadley zoomed off to join their family. Then Dannee and Dannill.

As I watched the reunions, my heart began to ache. My mom was probably worried sick. I'd been gone two whole days. The police might have given up looking for me by now.

I wanted to go home.

Tah-t-tah-TAH. A trumpet blew.

A wheat colored man dressed in a navy blue uniform called out, "His Majesty, King Davidius and Her Highness, Queen Unnowlio. Princess Salentia and Prince Sethadorian."

People backed up, leaving an aisle from the door to the thrones at the back of the room.

A tall, plum-colored giant entered. He had a golden crown on his head and wore a long white robe.

Walking beside him was another giant, magenta in color, who also wore a crown and a flowing white robe.

Behind them walked a young girl, young but still giant-sized. She was lavender and her head quills were gathered into two pink pigtails. Prince Seth stepped across the room so he could walk beside her.

Everyone cheered.

When the king and queen were on their thrones, Seth stood by his mother and his sister stood beside their father.

Tah-t-tah-TAH! Another trumpet blared.

The same man called out again, "His Majesty, King Stephenion and Her Highness, Queen Junitia. Princesses Letifiah and Cruzina."

In bounded two k'roll k'pollies, one saffron yellow and the other ginger brown. They wore silver circlets studded with gems on their heads and were dressed in matching blue jumpsuits. Following them, bounced two little girls. They were only slightly different shades of golden honey.

On a dais beside the thrones were two golden cushions. The k'roll k'pollie king and queen sat on them, and their little daughters stood on either side.

Everyone cheered again.

When people had quieted down, Prince Seth called me, Tashee, and the k'roll k'pollies forward. We lined up in a row and were presented to the kings and queens.

I was glad the others were introduced first or I wouldn't have known what to do. Unlike on earth, people don't bow or curtsy on Shalamar. If you'd ever seen a k'roll k'pollie, you'd understand why.

Tashee and the others simply extended their hands and then placed them over their hearts. So I did the same.

The monarchs acknowledged us with a nod.

Leaning forward, King Davidius told us, "On behalf of all the peoples of Shalamar, I want to thank you for your courage and ingenuity. You saved us from Groklan and his evil plans. In token of our appreciation, His Majesty, King Stephenion will present you each with the Emblem of Valor."

The k'roll k'pollie king leaped from the dais and bounced over to the wheat-colored official, who handed him a box.

From it, King Stephenion removed the awards, a golden circle hung from a navy blue ribbon. The king slipped one over each of our heads, and then returned to his cushion.

"Tomorrow, after you've had a good night's sleep," King Davidius said, "The High Fin, His Majesty All-White Paterick, has authorized Pink-Dotted Bertie to grant each of you a wish. Be thinking about what you'd like."

Then he threw his arms out wide.

"Let the festivities begin."

Chapter 30

The Heart's Desire

When the celebration began winding down, King Davidius invited the k'roll k'pollies who'd helped me and their families to spend the night in the palace. He arranged for rooms to be made ready.

Tashee stayed too, but she told me she had never slept inside a building before, except in Groklan's castle, which she had hated. She was used to sleeping in her rock.

No one knew what to do with her since there were no hollow rocks anywhere except in the swamp. Prince Seth offered to take her home on his magic carpet and call for her again in the morning, but she didn't want to be left out of whatever else might happen.

Finally Queen Unnowlio suggested Tashee might enjoy sleeping in the garden. In the middle of a large fountain was a lovely stone statue of a k'nick k'nocker girl holding a large empty pitcher on her shoulder.

Delighted, Tashee told everyone goodnight. She climbed the statue and curled up inside the jug.

For me, Prince Seth got a bed from his sister's dollhouse. He took it to his very own room and put it on a table beside his bed. Before I went to sleep, I asked him a question.

"Would your father be insulted if I asked him to send me home right after Pink-Dotted Bertie grants our wishes? I'm sure my mom is worried, and I really should get back to school. I've already ruined a perfect attendance record, and I missed a spelling test today."

"If I understand it correctly," Prince Seth said, "time moves differently on different worlds. Father may be able to send you home to the time you left. Maybe no one will need to know you were gone."

"Really? But I won't forget I was here, will I? I mean, I really did experience all this, didn't I?"

"Of course you did," Seth said. "You won't forget, and neither will we."

With that thought dancing through my head, I dozed off. The next thing I knew it was morning.

After having breakfast, the k'roll k'pollies, Tashee, and I were led back to the throne room.

King Davidius was on his throne, and a big, clear, fish bowl was on a table in front of him. Swimming in the bowl was the beautiful pink fish with the bright pink polka dots.

"Where's The High Fin?" asked Tashee. "I had hoped he'd be here too."

"His Majesty Paterick was exhausted from his captivity," the king said. "He's gone back to the swamp to recuperate. He's a very old fish, you know."

"Yes, your Majesty," Tashee said. "He was High Fin even when my grandmother was young."

"What would you like for your wish?" the king asked her.

"Well," Tashee said, "I've wanted my rock moved to a cooler part of the swamp, but since sleeping in your fountain, I've changed my mind. I'd like to have a statue like yours instead of a rock." She added quickly, "In the most pleasant part of the swamp, of course."

Pink-Dotted Bertie twirled and leaped in her bowl.

"Done." The king turned to Niklus. "What would you like?"

"I've already got my wish, your Majesty. I've got my family back."

"You don't want anything else?"

Niklus grinned. "Well, we did miss Grindlemach Day. Maybe a wham-k'bam pie. A huge one. Big enough to share."

Pink-Dotted Bertie splashed twice, and a pie as big around as

Niklus appeared on the floor at this feet.

"Wow. Thanks." Niklus's dad had to help him pick it up.

"I want one too," Jonthun said.

"Done."

Then Chadley, Jesska, Dannee, and Dannill each got a wish.

I was last, but I couldn't decide what I wanted.

"Do I get to keep the ring?" I asked.

"Of course," the king said. "It is yours now."

"Will its magic still work on Earth?"

"I'm sure it will. If it didn't work on your world, the ring couldn't have brought you here in the first place."

I thought and thought. "I know," I said. "I wish to take Mozart home with me."

"No," the king said, gently but firmly. "Fuzzle-wuzzles need to be around magic in order to be healthy. That's why they like fish-wishers so much. Unfortunately, the people on your planet have forgotten about magic, so it's become weak there. Too weak for a fuzzle-wuzzle to survive."

"I'll take care of him for you," said Tashee, sniffling and holding out her arms. Mozart, who'd been sitting on my shoulder, nuzzled my neck, and then leaped over to Tashee. He climbed up her arm, licked her face, and settled down on her shoulder. Even I could hear how loudly he was purring.

I sighed. What was left?

I've got it. "I wish to come back to Shalamar someday."

The king laughed. "No sense wasting a wish on that. The High Fin, Paterick, told me you would return."

"I don't know what to wish for then," I said. "The only other thing I want is to go home to my family, but Seth told me you were going to do that anyway."

"Surely there is something you want, something you didn't think you could ever have."

There was only one thing I wanted but couldn't have. I didn't know how to put it into words. Gradually it came to me.

"This is a little complicated," I said, "but I'd like to return home earlier than I left. After I picked up the ring, I fell into the creek and got all wet.

"I want to go back to when I first saw the ring. But when I put it on next time I don't want to come back here. I want to go to school without getting soaked. And I'll need my backpack, wherever it is.

"Of course, I don't want to change anything here. I want all of this to have happened, and I want to remember my new friends and the things we did together. Can you do that?"

"I can send you back to the exact moment you left," the king said, "but earlier? Altering time is difficult. I don't even know if The High Fin—"

A swirling red mist appeared in front of me. Floating inside it was the white fish I'd seen in the magic mirror.

The High Fin Paterick spoke to me. "I can grant your wish," he said. "But are you sure it is what you really want deep in your heart. I can give you anything. Gold and silver. Fame. Strength. Knowledge. Success. Love. I could make you the most powerful person on Earth."

I was tempted.

I could be taller. I could be as big as my brother, Sam, or even as big as Dad. No one would ever push me around again. But was that what I really wanted? Being big and strong and powerful hadn't made Groklan happy. All it had done was make him mean.

I shook my head.

"No, thank you. All I want is to go home with my backpack a few minutes earlier than when I left. And without changing anything that's happened here."

"Very well," Paterick told me. "Say goodbye to your friends."

Niklus and Jonthun, both a little sticky, tore themselves away from their wham-k'bam pies long enough to give me a hug. Chadley and Dannill shook my hand. Jesska and Dannee each gave me a little peck on the cheek.

Turning to Tashee, I didn't know what to say or do.

I think maybe she was the best friend I've ever had.

She threw her arms around my neck and kissed me square on the mouth. "You strange human from planet Earth, don't forget us," she said with a little catch in her voice.

"Never," was all I could manage to say.

My throat was all choked up.

I waved to Prince Seth and his father.

Then I nodded to The High Fin.

POOF!

Again.

A beam of yellow sunlight snuck around the clouds and flickered across the stream, making the water sparkle. Below the surface, I noticed something glittery.

Standing up, I put away my harmonica and pulled the straps of my backpack up over my shoulders.

With one foot on the bank and the other on a jagged rock, I bent and picked up a bright object.

The ring.

"What's that?" Buck Peterson shouted, jumping from behind the tree. His big, meaty fists tried to snatch the ring from me.

I could hardly believe my eyes.

I had thought Buck Peterson was big?

Heck, next to k'nick k'nockers and g'nome g'nasties, he was just a pygmy.

Slipping the ring onto my index finger, I said, "You want it, come get it."

"Why, you little runt." Buck lunged at me.

Left, I told the ring. I landed gracefully on the other side of the creek.

Kersplash! Buck Peterson fell face down in the water.

"Yes!" Raising my arms like an Olympic champion, I jumped in the air and yelled, "Yes, yes, yes!"

Then leaving Buck Peterson behind, I dashed off to school, only a few minutes late.

About the Author

Connie A. Walker has followed many paths on her journey to becoming a published author.

She has earned a Bachelor of Arts degree in theatre and playwriting from Brigham Young University and has had six original plays produced. She has a Bachelor of Science degree in psychology and a Master's degree in social work from the University of Utah.

She has worked as a psychotherapist, a foster care caseworker, and a clinical programs manager. She has been a technical writer, a graphic artist, a public relations specialist, a bookkeeper, and a secretary. She has lived in Kansas, Idaho, Alaska, and Utah.

Now retired, she is free to devote her time to writing.

The Spire of Kylet, a young adult fantasy, is the first book in The Wolkarean Inscription Trilogy. The protagonist, Katrine, is a fifteen-year-old girl who dreams of leaving home to become a Recorder, one of the elite historian/couriers who serve the Regent. After finding a spire, a magical weapon created three centuries earlier by the sorcerer Kylet, she performs an act of heroism. Suddenly, she is given powers she doesn't understand and faces a future she doesn't want. The second and third books in the trilogy, *The Eyes of Landor* and *Triumph at Serpent's Head,* will be available in 2011.

Connie is currently working on a second Wolkarean trilogy.

Another K'nick K'nocker book is in the planning stages.